Thoroughbred
Legacy

MILLIONS
TO SPARE

Barbara Dunlop

MILLS & BOON®
Pure reading pleasure™

First published in Great Britain 2009
by Harlequin Mills & Boon Limited,
Eton House, 18-24 Paradise Road, Richmond, Surrey TW9 1SR

Millions to Spare © Harlequin Books S.A. 2008

Special thanks and acknowledgement are given to Barbara Dunlop
for her contribution to the Thoroughbred Legacy series.

ISBN: 978 0 263 87170 8

61-0109

Harlequin Mills & Boon policy is to use papers that are
natural, renewable and recyclable products and made from
wood grown in sustainable forests. The logging and
manufacturing processes conform to the legal environmental
regulations of the country of origin.

Printed and bound in Spain
by Litografia Rosés S.A., Barcelona

Thoroughbred Legacy

The stakes are high

Scandal has hit the Preston family and their award-winning Quest Stables. Find out what it will take to return this horse racing dynasty to the winner's circle!

1. *Flirting with Trouble* by **Elizabeth Bevarly**
Publicist Marnie Roberts has just been handed a PR disaster that will bring her face-to-face with a gorgeous man from her past…

2. *Biding Her Time* by **Wendy Warren**
Audrey's "seize the day" attitude has thrown her into the arms of a straitlaced Aussie who doesn't do no-strings-attached!

3. *Picture of Perfection* by **Kristin Gabriel**
Sexy vet Carter Phillips has a tough choice to make – save his career at Quest or lose his heart to artist Gillian?

4. *Something to Talk About* by **Joanne Rock**
Widowed single mum Amanda Emory is hiding from her past, but Quest's trainer Robbie is ready to show her they could have a future.

5. *Millions to Spare* by **Barbara Dunlop**
Identifying with your captor is one thing. Marrying him is quite another! But that's just what reporter Julia is about to do…

6. *Courting Disaster* by **Kathleen O'Reilly**
Racing driver Demetri Lucas lives hard and fast – and he likes his women to match. Yet is Elizabeth up to the challenge?

Complete the collection next month with

000000725162

Dear Reader,

I love a story where a character is thrust out of her comfort zone. And what better place to strand a heroine than the vibrant, exotic, extraordinary world of the United Arab Emirates. Dubai: from glamorous skyscrapers by the sea to camels and sandstorms in the desert, nothing is familiar to journalist Julia Nash. She's arrested, then held captive by an English baron, then forced to flee for her life, all the while falling deeper in love with a completely inappropriate man.

I hope you enjoy Julia and Harrison's story. I was truly sorry the adventure had to end!

Barbara

BARBARA DUNLOP

is the bestselling, award-winning author of numerous novels for Mills & Boon. Her novels regularly hit bestseller lists for series romance, and she has twice been short-listed for the Romance Writers of America's RITA® Award.

Barbara lives in a log house in the Yukon Territory, where the bears outnumber the people, and moose graze in the front garden. By day, she works as the Yukon's Film Commissioner. By night, she pens romance novels in front of a roaring fire.

For Marsha Zinberg
With heartfelt thanks
for your encouragement and support

Chapter One

Julia Nash might hang out with the superrich, but she definitely wasn't one of them. She was only in Dubai because her employer, *Equine Earth Magazine,* had sent her there on assignment. And she was only staying at the Jumeirah Beach Hotel because her friend Melanie Preston, a jockey and the subject of the article, had insisted they share her room. Otherwise, Julia would have been down at the Crystal Sands, living within her reporter's travel allowance.

Like regular people, Julia had a condo payment, a crack in the windshield of her four-year-old Honda, and her eye on a limited edition watercolor at the Beauchamp Gallery back in Lexington. So, when Melanie had invited her shopping this afternoon, Julia decided not to subject herself to temptation. She'd claimed she was duty bound to scope out the Nad Al Sheba racecourse, and the excuse was mostly true. She needed to get a feel for the sights and sounds of the exotic Thoroughbred racecourse.

The Prestons owned Quest Stables outside Louisville, Kentucky, and their horse Something to Talk About would race in the Sandstone Derby on Thursday evening. Any background information Julia could pick up between now and then would make her story that much richer.

It was a fluff piece, something to combat the negative press the Prestons had received lately in connection with their Thoroughbred Leopold's Legacy. DNA tests had revealed that the stallion was not sired by Apollo's Ice, as recorded, and therefore could no longer compete in Thoroughbred races until the true sire was found. But she took the job seriously. Not only were the Prestons her friends and in need of positive publicity, Julia knew her way out of the lifestyle section of *Equine Earth* was to do each and every story to the best of her ability.

Although today's Thoroughbred races wouldn't start for a couple of hours, the Arabian and expatriate crowd was beginning to gather. Men in white robes contrasted with women in high fashion. Grooms walked sleek horses, while jockeys chatted amongst themselves, some suited up, some still in street clothes.

In the three years she'd been working for *Equine Earth,* Julia had developed an appreciation for Thoroughbreds and their breeding. She even imagined she was developing an eye for which horse had potential and which one did not. She'd never be as good at it as Melanie, who'd grown up at her family's famous racing stables. And she couldn't touch Melanie's brother Robbie, Something to Talk About's trainer.

But, for now, she slowed to watch two horses pass by on the dirt track on the opposite side of the fence from her, judging for herself the Thoroughbred's potential. It was easy to tell which was the helper and which was the racer. One was a stocky, barrel-bellied chestnut with a scraggly black mane, who looked positively bombproof. The other was a twitchy, long-legged dun, straining at the halter, its tail flicking nervously over its haunches.

Wait a minute.

Julia inched toward the fence, straining for a closer look at the tail. The Thoroughbred was a dun. It had a clover-shaped star and the familiar, dark-brown eyes. It also had that unique flaxen tail that Julia had stared at in dozens of pictures at the Prestons.

The Prestons' veterinarian, Carter Phillips, had found a stallion in California two months ago that he swore was a twin to Leopold's Legacy. Julia realized she had now found a triplet.

She paced alongside the animal, trying to keep up without looking conspicuous. She scanned its head, its shoulders, its withers and legs, desperately searching her brain for something definitive, something that would tell her whether this was an animal worth investigating. She wished her eye was as keen as Melanie's or Robbie's.

Then, she remembered her cell phone. Perfect. She'd e-mail a picture to Melanie and take it from there.

All but trotting along under the warmth of a waning desert sun, she dug into her small purse, tugging out her cell phone. Then she ran a couple of steps to get the angle right, and held up the phone.

Instantly, a white, brass-buttoned, uniformed chest stepped between her and the fence, blocking her view.

"I am very sorry, madam," the man said, not looking sorry at all.

Julia had no choice but to stop. She tipped her head to blink into a dark, bearded face, shaded by a peaked cap.

"No pictures," he informed her, his lips clamped in a stern line.

"I don't understand," she lied, glancing around, cursing the fact that the horse was getting away.

The No Photos signs were posted conspicuously around the racetrack in at least six languages—three of which Julia spoke.

"No pictures," the man repeated. "And this is not a public area."

She maintained her facade of confusion, still keeping an eye on the retreating dun. "But—"

"I must ask you to return to the stands." The man gestured back the way she'd come.

She peeked around him one last time, scrambling for a solution before the horse and groom disappeared. "Do you know who owns that horse?" she asked.

"This is not a public area," the man repeated.

"I just need to know—"

Suddenly, a rugged-looking man in a white head scarf and a flowing, white robe materialized beside them. "Do we have a problem?"

Julia instinctively took a step back, shaking her head in denial that she was causing any kind of a problem. This did not look like the kind of man she wanted to annoy. His beard was scraggly, the tip of his nose was missing, and one eyebrow was markedly shorter than the other. Truly, she had no desire to run afoul of somebody who looked like a bar-fight veteran.

"I was only..." She took another step back, taking

note of the primal urge that told her to put some distance between the two of them. "Curious about a horse."

His eyes narrowed. "Which horse?"

"The dun. I..." She hesitated, then screwed up her courage. If she walked away now, she might never find out about the horse, and she might lose a real opportunity to help the Prestons.

She gave her eyelashes a determined flutter and offered a bright, ingenuous grin. "It's pretty. When's it racing?"

His thin lips curved into a cold smile. "You wish to bet?"

"No. No, of course I don't want to bet." Betting was illegal in Dubai.

"He is Millions to Spare. The third race."

A name. She had a name. Julia mentally congratulated herself.

She turned to leave, but the man's hand closed around her upper arm. She glanced down, spotting a tiny tattoo on his inner wrist. It was square, red and gold, with a diagonal line cut through the center.

"You talk to Al Amine," the man said.

She struggled not to panic.

But then he released her. "For a bet. You talk to Al Amine."

She reflexively glanced at the uniformed man. Either his English was weak, or they didn't take the no-betting law particularly seriously around here.

In either event, Julia had the Thoroughbred's name. A little more sleuthing, and she'd have the name of the stable. If luck was with her, she could end up with more than a fluff piece from this trip. Imagine if she was able to solve the mystery, identify Leopold's Legacy's true sire? The Prestons would be in the clear, and her name would be on a byline.

Since earning her journalism degree at Cal State, she'd dreamed of breaking significant news stories, of bringing insights and information to millions of readers around the world. So far, she'd only managed to bring insights on horse racing to a limited audience through *Equine Earth.*

Not that *Equine Earth* was a bad employer; they had brought a lower middle-class Seattle girl all the way to Dubai. And soon she'd have enough experience and credentials to branch out to harder news, maybe with a mainstream publication.

As the crowds closed in behind her, she took one last glance at the mystery stallion.

"Come on, Leopold's Legacy connection," she muttered under her breath. For the first time in her career, a racehorse story had the potential to move beyond the business and into the mainstream.

Through the speakers above her, the announcer switched from English to Arabic to Spanish, reciting some of the more prominent horses' names and the time left to the first parade to the post.

Julia ignored the growing excitement in the audience. Her goal was information on Millions to Spare. If she could find a program, she could look up the name of his stable and potentially be on her way to a significant story.

Cadair Racing.

The lettering on the side of the eight-horse trailer was in both English and Arabic. There was a phone number beneath, but a telephone call was the last thing on Julia's mind. Millions to Spare was in that trailer. And Julia was in the middle of an honest-to-God covert operation here.

She'd figured out the one thing, the one little thing that would tell her for certain if Millions to Spare was a lead in the Leopold's Legacy parentage mystery, or just another dead end. And that little thing was his DNA.

She'd watched men load the stallion into the eight-horse trailer just a few minutes ago. Now, the last groom was walking away, leaving it unattended, and providing Julia with her golden chance.

Carter Phillips had run into nothing but resistance when he'd checked out the DNA of the other Leopold's Legacy look-alike in California. His experience had taught Julia it was better to ask for forgiveness than permission. Considering her DNA test might result in Millions to Spare being disqualified from the Thoroughbred registry, she wasn't about to call Cadair in advance. She was going to gather the facts first, then deal with the implications—if there were any—later.

All she needed was a tiny sample. Millions to Spare wouldn't even miss it. Then Carter Phillips could run the test, and she'd know if she had a live investigation on her hands, or if she was switching back to the straight fluff piece about the Prestons' two-year-old Something to Talk About racing in Dubai.

She took a final glance around the parking lot. Seeing no one who appeared interested in the Cadair Racing trailer, she scooted out in high-heeled sandals, a sleeveless white blouse and a straight, linen skirt. It was hardly the right outfit to go sleuthing around a horse trailer, but she couldn't let that slow her down.

She tested the handle on the small side door. The silver metal was smooth and warm on her palm. To her relief, the door opened easily.

Heart pounding, she swung it wide and slipped into the cloying dimness, quickly clicking the door shut behind her. She took a deep breath, then sneezed out a gulp of hay dust, startling the closest horse.

There were five of them in the trailer. There were also three empty stalls, and she realized the grooms could be back at any moment with more horses. She couldn't waste any time. She took shallow breaths to keep from sneezing as she wound her way between oiled saddles, hanging bridles, black water buckets and prickly hay bales.

It was going to be easy, she assured herself. She'd seen this particular test done on television dozens of times. On humans, of course. But the principle was the same.

She had a small cosmetics bag in her purse. All she needed to do was run one of the cotton swabs over Millions to Spare's gums and wrap it in the plastic she'd obtained from the café. Then she'd slip back out the side door and send the sample by FedEx to Carter Phillips in Kentucky. By Thursday, and the running of the Sandstone Derby, they'd have their answer. And, with luck, she'd be writing a fantastic story.

She squinted at the horses, trying to ignore the sticky sweat dampening her blouse. The horse in the farthest corner whinnied and shuffled, bouncing the trailer. Then there was a clanging of hooves as another horse reacted to the disturbance.

Julia identified Millions to Spare and made her move, murmuring low as she passed the helper mare. She crouched under the barrier, then, moving steadily, she passed another Thoroughbred in the middle stall. She came abreast of Millions to Spare and patted him on the shoulder as she spoke.

"Good horse." Pat, pat, pat.

"I'm just going to…" her sweaty hands slipped on the clasp of her leather purse "…take a little test of your saliva. It won't hurt a bit."

She pawed her way past her wallet, lipstick, comb and a little loose change. The Thoroughbred in front of Millions to Spare twitched. Julia automatically shrank back, her stomach clamping down and her mouth going dry. A kick in here could cause a disaster.

Finally, she located the cosmetic bag and her cotton swabs.

"We can do this," she crooned to the horse. "You and me, Millions to Spare. Then nice Dr. Phillips will tell us who your father is."

She carefully inched her fingers along the horse's cheek, pulling gently on the bottom lip, stroking the cotton along his gums.

Millions to Spare snorted and pulled his head away.

But Julia had succeeded.

She carefully wrapped the swab then tucked it back in her purse, giving Millions to Spare a final pat. "Good boy."

Just then, the truck's diesel engine rumbled to life.

The horses all shifted, shaking the trailer, and pitching Julia into the wall.

Sucking in a breath, she pushed herself back to standing. She ducked under the barrier, coming abreast of the middle Thoroughbred. Intent on the side door, she was determined to jump out before the truck got rolling. As long as no one happened to be looking in the rear-view mirror, she'd be free and clear.

But the middle horse shifted again, canting its hip, knocking Julia sideways and pinning her in a groove of the molded metal wall.

An unladylike swearword burst out of her, and she scrambled to regain her footing.

She gave the horse a firm shove.

It didn't budge.

She shoved harder.

The trailer lurched and rolled forward.

Julia smacked the horse sharply on the rump.

It shook its head, but its hindquarters stayed planted against the center of her chest.

Panic threatened, but she fought it down.

She could breathe. Sure, they were moving now, but they would have to stop soon. There'd be intersections and red lights between here and Cadair Racing. All she had to do was get free and make her way to the side door.

Then she'd wait for an opportunity, hop out and hail a cab.

She groaned, shoving impatiently at the horse's rump one more time.

Nothing.

Okay. Deep breath. This wasn't a disaster. It was just your typical investigative reporter stuff. She'd be laughing about it later tonight with Melanie and Robbie—over a glass of Merlot and a really big lobster tail. Thank goodness alcohol was tolerated in the international hotels in Dubai, because she was going to need it after this experience. The Thoroughbred's hip bone was leaving a mark.

The bumps and bruises of polo made it a young man's sport.

Not that Lord Harrison Rochester was old. And at

age thirty-five, he wasn't ready to give up polo just yet. But as he watched from the sidelines, Jamal Fariol galloped fearlessly down the field at Ghantoot, close to the line, bent nearly sideways in his effort to turn the play. Harrison involuntarily cringed. Another inch and the boy would go tumbling under the hooves of his opponent's horse.

But Jamal didn't lose his seat. He connected with the ball and pulled up on his reins. There was a cheer of relief from the crowd as the ball bounced its way down the field and the horn sounded.

Harrison watched the young men sit smooth in their saddles—strong and eager as they headed for the side-lines, a new generation full of energy and idealism. His grandmother's words echoed insistently in his mind.

"Brittany Livingston is the one," she'd said for the hundredth time. "I know it. What's more, you know it yourself." She'd shaken a wrinkled finger in Harrison's eyes. "Mark my words, young man, you'll regret it to your dying day if you let someone else swoop in while you dillydally around."

Harrison had responded that he wasn't ready to settle down and have children with Brittany or anyone else. He acknowledged that marriage was his duty. But he reminded her that duty came after the fun was over, and Harrison was still having plenty of fun.

Still, as he watched the boys on the field this evening, he couldn't help thinking about children and father-hood and his own mortality. If he was going to have children anyway, he might want to do it while he was young enough to enjoy them.

Jamal was fourteen now, his father, Hanif, only a few years older than Harrison. On the sidelines, Hanif's face shone with pride as he watched his son gallop off the field to switch horses between chukkers. The lad was limping from an earlier fall, but he gamely leaped up on the new mount.

"Impressive," said Harrison, speculating, probably for the first time, on the pride of fatherhood.

"Kareem is the same," Hanif offered, his chest puffing as he referred to his twelve-year-old son. "Both of them. Robust like me."

"That they are," Harrison agreed, toying with the image of Brittany's face. There was no denying she was attractive. She had a sweet smile, crystal-blue eyes and a crown of golden hair. She was also kind and gentle, a preschool teacher. There's wasn't a single doubt she'd make a wonderful mother.

The match started up again, hooves thudding, divots flying, the crowd shouting encouragement.

Testing the idea further, Harrison conjured up a picture of Brittany in a veil and a white dress, walking the nave at St. Paul's. He could see his grandmother's smile and his mother's joy.

Then he imagined the two of them making babies. He'd have to be careful not to hurt her. Unlike Hanif's sons, nobody would describe Brittany as robust. It would be sweet, gentle sex, under a lace canopy, beneath billowing white sheets, Brittany's fresh face smiling up at him—for the rest of his natural life.

Which wouldn't be so bad.

A man could certainly do worse.

And there was a lot Harrison could teach sons or daughters, not to mention the perfectly good title he had to pass on.

Jamal scored, and Hanif whooped with delight.

Harrison clapped Hanif's shoulder in congratulations. Making up his mind, he pulled out his cell phone and pressed number one on his speed dial.

"Cadair Racing," came the immediate answer.

"Darla please."

"Right away, Lord Rochester."

A moment later, his assistant Darla's voice came through the speaker amidst the lingering cheers of the crowd. "Can I help you, sir?"

"I'd like to add a couple of names to the guest list."

"Of course."

Harrison's stomach tightened almost imperceptibly. But it was time. And, fundamentally, Brittany was a good choice. "My grandmother and Brittany Livingston. There shouldn't be any security concerns."

"Certainly. I'll send out the invitations right away. By the way, the French ambassador accepted this morning, and so did Colonel Varisco."

"That's great. So are they back?"

"The horses are en route now. Ilithyia placed and Millions to Spare won."

"Not bad," said Harrison, nodding to himself.

"Brittany Livingston?" asked Darla, the lilt of her voice seeking confirmation, even though she knew full well what the invitation had to mean. In her midthirties, single, yet hopelessly romantic, Darla made no bones about the fact she thought Harrison should find a suitable wife.

"You think it's a bad idea?" he asked, remembering Darla singing the praises of Yvette Gaston from the French embassy only last week.

"I think it's an excellent idea," said Darla with clear enthusiasm.

"Yes. Well. So will Grandmother."

"And you?" Darla probed.

"How could I go wrong?"

"How, indeed. A beautiful hostess improves any party."

Harrison's stomach protested once again. But he supposed being his hostess was exactly what he was asking Brittany to do. "Millions to Spare won, you say?" He redirected Darla.

There was a trace of laughter in her voice when she answered. "The purse was six figures."

"Tell Nuri to give that boy some oats."

"Mr. Nuri!" The teenager's round dark eyes fixed disbelievingly on Julia where she stood frozen in the corner of the horse trailer.

Sweat prickled her skin, and her heart threatened to beat its way out of her chest. With her back pressed against the warm metal wall, she attempted to swallow her fear, telling herself she should have made a run for it when they first arrived.

"Quiet down," came a harsh, heavily accented voice from outside the near-empty horse trailer. Stern footsteps clomped up the ramp.

A tall, brawny, dark-haired man appeared. He wore a turban and a black robe, and he carried a riding crop. His piercing eyes took in Julia, and then shifted to the teenager. Then he was back to Julia before rattling something off in Arabic.

The teenage boy scuttled from the trailer.

"I'm sorry," Julia rasped, straightening away from the wall, moving toward him, frantically scrambling for a cover story. "It's just. Well. I was—"

The butt of his crop landed square in her chest, forcing a cry from her lips and sending her stumbling back.

"Save it for the authorities," he grated.

Chapter Two

"An intruder?" From behind the desk in his study at Cadair Racing, Harrison stared at Alex Lindley—lawyer and senior vice president of Cadair International.

"An American," said Lindley, dropping down into the diamond-tuft leather chair, next to the potted palm trees and the bay window that looked out across Harrison's lighted lawn. "The police have arrested her."

"And she was hiding in my horse trailer?" The pieces of Alex's story weren't coming together in any sort of coherent order inside Harrison's head.

The only thing certain was that he had trouble.

The United Nations International Economic Summit was only four days away, and Harrison was hosting the secretary-general's reception here at Cadair. Surprises couldn't happen at this stage of the game.

"Nuri thought she was stealing a horse," said Alex. "But she insisted she was a reporter."

"What? Was she interviewing Ilithyia?"

Alex choked out a laugh. "Didn't seem likely. That's why Nuri called the police."

Good move on Nuri's part. Reporters knocked on the front door. They didn't sneak onto the estate in the back of a horse trailer. Unless they were from a tabloid. And since Harrison wasn't a movie star, and there was nothing remotely salacious going on at Cadair Racing, this could hardly be an exposé.

Then Harrison's brain hit on a worst-case scenario.

"Son of a bitch," he all but shouted.

"She can't be," said Alex, correctly interpreting the outburst.

"Sure she can," said Harrison.

There was no reason in the world the woman couldn't be attached to a foreign spy agency or black-ops organization.

"A covert operative in a horse trailer?"

"It got her past security."

"She's an American," Alex pointed out. "The CIA doesn't have anything against the UN."

"Yeah? Well, they've got something against the Syrians and the Iranians."

"That's a stretch."

"Maybe. But that's bizarre behavior for a horse thief, and she's certainly not here to do a feature on my love life for the *National Inquisitor.*"

The grandfather clock ticked three times before Alex spoke. "You want me to head down to the lockup and sleuth around?"

Harrison pushed back on his chair and came to his

feet. "No. I'll get her. If she *is* an assassin, it's my neck on the line."

"We could leave her locked up until the reception's over. She can't hurt anyone from jail."

"That only works if she's acting alone."

Alex went silent as Harrison stood up, pressing a hidden button to reveal a wall safe.

"Jobar's on duty," Alex warned.

"It figures," Harrison grumbled. He spun the dial back and forth then clunked the lever. He pulled out three stacks of bills.

Jobar was usually expensive. If the woman *was* CIA, Harrison hoped the American government would consider reimbursing his bribe.

Julia had to get out of jail.

She had to get *out of this cell,* and then she had to pee.

Okay. Not necessarily in that order.

The need had been growing steadily worse for the past two hours, but neither of the hijab-clad women spoke English, Spanish *or* French, and her sign-language repertoire didn't extend to urination.

There was a drain in the middle of the sloping stone floor. Crude. But it was looking better and better all the time.

She could be discreet.

She was alone in the cell. And it wasn't as if she still had her underwear. And the voluminous gray dress they'd forced on her was essentially a tent with sleeves. It was drab and scratchy, with a musky smell that made her gag. But it would certainly hide her activities.

Of course, the drain might not be the toilet. In which

case, she might be committing some horrible faux pas. She might even be breaking another law. They'd already added immodest dress to her charges of break-in and attempted theft.

And they hadn't let her make a phone call. In fact, they'd confiscated her cell phone along with every other one of her possessions. She'd repeated the words *American* and *embassy* until she was nearly hoarse. She could only hope someone had called them.

If not...

She glanced around at the stained cement walls and the iron-barred door, shivering despite the close air. Voices shouted down the narrow hallway, and metal clanked in the distance. A centipede wriggled out from under the bare mattress laid across the floor.

Julia shuddered, swallowing a shriek.

Why had she thought she could be a real reporter? Why had she ever left Seattle? She should have taken that promotion to night-shift supervisor at Econo Foods instead of the scholarship to Cal State and the road that brought her to *this*.

She had to keep it together, she told herself firmly. Melanie and Robbie must be looking for her. They'd have talked to the authorities by now. Eventually, hopefully within the next few hours, they'd find her and contact the embassy. Surely getting trapped in a horse trailer wasn't a heinous crime even in Dubai.

Oh, God. She had to pee.

She gritted her teeth, lowering herself onto one corner of the mattress then bending over to keep her muscles tight.

Footfalls sounded in the corridor. An Arabic voice again. But this time a man's.

"Ms. Nash?"

She jerked her head up to see a tall man standing outside her cell door. He was Caucasian. And he spoke English. Thank goodness.

"Are you from the embassy?" she rasped.

He shook his head. "I'm afraid not."

Her need was humiliating. But she was past caring. She couldn't even think about anything else for the moment. "Is there a bathroom?"

He searched her expression then said something in rapid Arabic to the matron beside him.

The matron unlocked the door, and Julia rushed to the opening. The woman then escorted Julia down the hall.

The restroom was a cramped, dingy stall with cracked porcelain and corrosion-encrusted plumbing that was a relic of the fifties. There was no seat, and toilet paper didn't appear to be one of the amenities. But Julia had never seen anything so beautiful in her life.

Afterward, she thanked the stern, cold-eyed woman then walked back down the hall, pulling together the few shreds of dignity she could muster.

The man still stood outside her cell.

Her feet froze at the doorway, everything inside her screaming to break and run. But she knew that would only make matters worse. She forced her rational mind to override her primal instincts.

"You speak English," she said, still hovering at the open doorway.

"I'm British," he responded.

Of course. The accent was obvious. And there was a definite aristocratic look about him. He had a straight nose, a slight cleft to his square chin, and dark eyes that matched his neatly trimmed hair. His suit was Armani, the shirt and tie likely Richard James. Whoever he was, he had money and style.

She shifted, more conscious than ever of her drab dress. They'd scrubbed off all her makeup, and her hair had definitely suffered from the wind whipping through the openings in the horse trailer.

"The British embassy?" she asked. Perhaps the Americans were busy.

"Harrison Rochester." His pause was definitely for effect, and he watched her closely as he delivered the next sentence. "I own Cadair Racing."

For the first time in several hours, a spurt of anger overtook her despair. It was this man's fault she'd been manhandled, humiliated and strip-searched. "*You* had me arrested?"

He considered her for a short second. "*You* broke into my stable."

"It was an accident." She sure hadn't meant to travel halfway across the United Arab Emirates pinned to the side of a horse trailer.

He eyed her with suspicion. "You mistook my trailer for the loo?"

She could feel her face flush, and she tried not to squirm under his intent scrutiny.

She had only a split second to decide how much to tell him. The truth might give her the best chance of getting out of jail. Then again, if she told him she was trying to discredit his racehorse in advance of the Sandstone Derby, he might be tempted to leave her right where she was.

"I was after a story," she told him. She could always elaborate later.

His slate gaze locked with her blue one. "In my horse trailer?"

"I liked your horses."

"You're lying."

"Check my credentials," she countered, her confidence growing, since everything she was about to tell him was the truth. "I work for *Equine Earth Magazine*."

His eyes narrowed. "I will."

"Good."

He glanced back into her cell, and it was all she could do not to beg him to help her, to please call *Equine Earth* right here and now. Or, better still, take her with him while he checked out her credentials. Just don't, please don't let them put her back with the rank air and the centipedes.

She knew they'd turn off the lights soon. And she wouldn't be able to see the bugs. And, the truth was, she was kind of wimpy for an investigative reporter—especially when it came to creepy-crawly things.

She swallowed and waited.

His broad hand reached out and latched on to one of the iron bars, bracing him beside her. He stared down for a moment. Then he took a breath. "They've agreed to release you into my custody."

Relief burst through her, along with an urge to throw herself into his arms. Her elation must have shown, because his frown deepened.

"You're not out of the woods yet," he warned. "You're in *my* custody. I'm keeping your passport, and you'll not be permitted to leave Cadair until I figure out who you are and what you're about."

Julia quickly nodded her agreement.

Her story would check out. Harrison would discover

she was a bona fide reporter, and he'd have no reason to suspect she was after anything other than a human-interest story.

Meanwhile, if they gave her back her purse, she'd still have the DNA sample and a chance of getting it to the lab. Plus, the Cadair staff might know something about Millions to Spare's history. Hanging around and talking to them for a few hours could be a blessing in disguise.

Besides—she glanced around at the mottled white walls while resisting the urge to rip the gray dress from her body—whatever conditions they kept her in at Cadair Racing, it had to be a damn sight better than this.

As it turned out, the palace at Cadair Racing was about as far from a prison cell as a person could get. Harrison was definitely one of the superrich. He easily surpassed the Prestons and pretty much anybody else Julia had ever met in the horse world.

A huge, multistoried, marble-pillared rotunda served as his entryway. It was decorated with gilt mirrors, antique statues and hand-carved mahogany settees. A painted mural dominated the domed ceiling, while chandeliers, suspended on gold chains, fairly dripped with glowing crystal.

Past a center table that boasted a massive fresh flower arrangement, the tiled mosaic floor opened into a wide hallway. The hallway itself was an oil painting gallery, inviting guests to browse their way through the center of the palace. Doorways to the left and the right revealed a library, several sitting rooms, an office and an arboretum.

Growing up with her widowed father in a Seattle suburb, Julia hadn't crossed paths with the wealthy.

She knew they lived on the lakefront and went to private schools in Bellevue. Other than that, she'd always assumed they were just like her, but with pools and chauffeurs.

Not true.

When she'd started hanging out with the Thorough-bred racing crowd, she'd learned the rich were closed-minded and paranoid. One racehorse owner refused to eat anything that wasn't from France. Another put an armed guard on his poodle. Yet another was rumored to carry a briefcase full of hundred-dollar bills, in case he wanted to make an untraceable purchase.

It seemed to Julia that the richer people were, the stranger they became. Given this house and its furnish-ings, along with the extensive grounds and security, Harrison was saddled with a lot of eccentricities.

The end of the wide passage opened into a great hall. The room boasted sweeping staircases, along with banks of windows and glass doors that led to a veranda overlooking a lighted, emerald lawn. Scattered palm trees waved their way to a white sand beach that met the rolling azure waters of the Persian Gulf.

"I really need to make a phone call," Julia told him, feeling more than a little self-conscious in her stained skirt and wrinkled white blouse as the crisply dressed, ubiqui-tous staff members moved silently through the rooms.

"I'm afraid I can't let you do that," Harrison re-sponded as they made their way toward the veranda.

Julia kept her voice even, determined not to let her nervousness show. "I don't understand. Why not?"

He stopped and turned to look down at her. "Because I don't know who you are, or what you're after or who you'll call."

She glanced pointedly to where her small purse was tucked under his arm. "You've seen my passport, my driver's license, my Lexington *library card*."

He didn't respond.

"People will start to worry," she pointed out. Hopefully Melanie was worried already. "They'll be out looking for me."

Harrison paused. "Give me a list of names. I'll have Darla make the calls."

It was Julia's turn to hesitate. She didn't want him connecting her with the Prestons. He might have heard about the Leopold's Legacy scandal, and he might already know Millions to Spare was the spitting image. Melanie and Robbie's names could give her away.

Harrison arched a brow. "Problem?"

She stalled. "What's she going to say to them?"

"That you're safe."

"You don't think they'll ask questions?"

A sly smile grew on his face. "She can tell them you met a man."

Annoyance shot through Julia. "You think my friends are going to believe I *came home* with you?"

"Why not? You're a modern, twenty-five-year-old American—"

"Watch it, buster." Sure, there was a social conduct divide between the East and the West, but that didn't mean she was sleazy.

He slowly perused her sleeveless blouse, short skirt and high-heeled shoes. "I saw your *personal* effects, remember?"

"You think because I wear a thong I'll jump into bed with a man I just met?" Of all the insulting, stereotypical assumptions. She wore a thong today to stay cool, because the weather in Dubai was nearly a hundred degrees.

He moved a little closer, lowering his voice. "I think your underwear was designed to share."

She moved in closer, as well, glaring defiantly into his slate-gray eyes. "Not with an insufferable bastard like you."

His mild tone belied the mocking glint in his eyes. "But, Julia. Since your friends have never met me, they won't know I'm an insufferable bastard, will they?"

Even though logic told her to back off, there was something about his smug smile that begged her to retaliate. "*I'll* know."

"Guess I'll just have to live with your low opinion," he said, clearly unperturbed by the insult. "Give Darla the list. I promise she'll convince your friends you're having the time of your life."

She kept her mouth firmly shut.

His expression unexpectedly softened. "We can end all this right now, Julia. Just tell me why you're here."

"I'm doing a human-interest story for *Equine Earth Magazine*."

"On me."

"Yes."

"Yet, you didn't recognize me at the jail. Didn't look at a picture before you broke in?"

Julia scrambled for an explanation. "You look different in real life."

Harrison laughed at that one. "You're really the best they could find?"

They? "Who?"

His cell phone buzzed, and he shook his head as he pulled it out. "Never mind."

"One moment," he said into the phone, then he snapped his fingers. A young woman instantly responded to the summons, reminding Julia that Harrison was king here, and his word was law.

"Leila will show you to your room," he said. "She'll provide you with clothing, food and anything else you need." His nod was curt as he turned away to deal with the phone call.

The young woman smiled shyly at Julia, and suddenly the prospect of clean clothes and something to eat overruled everything, even the need to bring überrich Harrison down a peg or two.

"Thank you," she said to Leila, genuinely grateful for the young woman's help.

Leila gestured to one of the staircases. "This way, please."

"You speak English?"

"Yes, ma'am."

"Is there a phone I could use?"

Leila looked uncomfortable. "I'm afraid not, ma'am."

Julia sighed. She shouldn't have been surprised the staff had been given instructions about her. Harrison definitely struck her as a detail-oriented kind of guy.

At the top of the staircase, her feet sank into the thick carpet of the hallway as they made their way along an open railing that looked down into the atrium.

Julia didn't know whether to admire or sneer at the tall trees and the broad-leaved tropical plants below and the brilliant starscape through the domed glass ceiling above. It was all gorgeous, but definitely excessive.

When Leila opened a set of double doors, the opulence of the suite echoed that excess all over again.

A four-poster bed dominated the room, while a plush furniture grouping was tucked into an alcove. The carpet was as luxurious as the one in the hall, potted plants were dotted all around, and a door led to an absolutely decadent marble en suite with an oversize tub, gold faucets and double sinks.

Although the silly gold faucets were probably worth more than her car, Julia had to admit it was a whole lot better than her last prison cell. And, really, with a palace this big, there had to be an unguarded telephone somewhere.

Chapter Three

"So is she a spy?" asked Alex Lindley, stopping in the doorway of Harrison's study, a snifter of cognac dangling from his fingers.

Harrison kept his gazed fixed on the Web page on his computer monitor. "It would appear a Julia Nash does, indeed, work for *Equine Earth Magazine*. Of course, it might not be our Julia Nash. And, even if it is, it could be a cover."

Alex moved into the room. "A fake identity as a reporter would give her an excuse to travel around the world."

Harrison nodded. He'd also found several dozen horse-themed articles written by Julia Nash, a scientific paper by a professor of the same name, a Julia Nash on the board of directors of Qantas Communications

Company, and a couple of genealogy charts naming long-deceased Julia Nashes.

His quick search hadn't come up with anything that either convicted or exonerated her. It might mean she was an innocent reporter or it might mean she was simply a competent covert operative—since none of them would have their real profession splashed all over the Internet, either.

Alex glanced over Harrison's shoulder. "You want me to make a couple of calls to my military contacts?"

As an American ex-naval officer, Alex could still call in favors in most countries in the world.

"All that will do is send up one mother of a red flag in the secretary-general's office," said Harrison.

"Yeah," Alex agreed. "Might as well cancel the reception outright as do that."

Harrison pushed back in his chair. "And we won't be canceling the reception."

Alex nodded his agreement. As Harrison's right-hand man, he knew full well the real reason behind the reception. It would facilitate under-the-radar consultations on an international oil pipeline.

"You hear anything more on the negotiations?" asked Alex.

"Uzbekistan's on board, of course. But Kazakhstan can't move without a Russian security guarantee. That means Turkmenistan has the French over a barrel on financing."

"No French, no financing."

"No port access and no pipeline." Harrison finished what they both knew.

"If it all goes to hell, what kind of a loss are you looking at?" asked Alex.

"Sunk capital or net present value."

"I don't even want to *think* about net present value."

"A hundred million in drilling anyway."

Alex whistled under his breath. "Then I guess we won't be sending up any red flags for the secretary-general's security staff, will we?"

Harrison gave a nod to that. Russia wasn't going to budge on their position on the pipeline. And if the secretary-general canceled his attendance at the reception, the high-level diplomats would follow suit. Harrison would lose his one chance for a meaningful conversation between the French, the Uzbeks and the Turkmen.

At the same time, if Julia Nash was some kind of an operative, or if she wasn't working alone, and managed to pull something off at the reception, he could trigger one hell of an international incident.

"So what do we do?" asked Alex, dropping down into a guest chair.

"Beef up security," said Harrison. "Talk to her. See if I can get a feel for…" He swung to his feet, searching for the right words. "I don't know. But she doesn't strike me as…"

"The best spies never do," said Alex.

Harrison frowned at his friend. He knew that. But he'd also been around international commerce and politics long enough to get a feel for people. He was usually right in his assessments.

Then again, the stakes weren't usually quite this high.

"I'll talk to her again," he repeated.

"If you're sure," said Alex.

"It's my ass in a sling."

"Unless the bullets start flying. Then it's all of our asses."

Harrison gave a hard sigh. "I lose a hundred million in sunk costs," he said to Alex.

"Then you'd better talk to her."

Harrison glanced at the clock. They'd passed midnight a couple of hours ago. "Let's hope she doesn't plan to sleep late."

The next morning, it took Julia a few minutes to orient herself. Her eyes blinked open to bright sunshine, and the bed beneath her was incredibly soft and comfortable. A window was open, and the cool morning air wafted over her comforter, bringing with it the sound of birds and scents of jasmine and roses.

But then she remembered.

Her white, embroidered cotton nightgown was borrowed, and there was a lock on the outside of her door. After marveling for a brief moment over her sound sleep under such frustrating conditions, she dragged back her covers and headed for the bathroom. She had no idea what the day would bring, and she wanted to be ready.

She showered, then discovered that somebody—she assumed it was Leila—had left a simple, cowl-neck dress of ice-blue silk on the freshly made bed. It had three-quarter-length sleeves, a wide, gauzy hood that could be pulled up as a head scarf, and it fell to just below her knees. Whoever it was had also left a pair of practical, low-heeled sandals that hugged Julia's feet softly as she tested them on the carpeted floor.

Then she opened the French doors and walked onto the third-floor balcony, gazing at the stables and the sea beyond, giving herself the illusion of freedom.

A rap sounded on the door. She assumed it would be Leila or maybe breakfast, but she didn't bother going back inside to answer it. People seemed to come and go as they pleased around here.

Sure enough, the door swung open without her help.

It was Leila, and she carried a silver tray of coffee, fruit and pastries. The scrolled tray was further decorated with a small bouquet of flowers, as if Julia cared about opulent hospitality.

Leila was followed by Harrison, looking stern and forbidding in a dark business suit. Julia had to admit the man would be considered handsome, even sexy by most. Not that she was into self-assured, self-absorbed powermongers.

Still, she gave herself a quick lecture on the dangers of falling for your captor—Stockholm syndrome—just in case he started looking good.

"Thank you," she said to Leila, advancing back into the room as the woman set the tray down on a low table between the two armchairs and the love seat. It occurred to Julia that she should probably stand on principle and refuse to eat her jailer's food. Part of her wanted to be that defiant, but another part urged her to be practical. A debate ping-ponged through her brain as Leila let herself out of the room.

"You need to eat," came Harrison's deep voice.

She glanced up to see him gesturing at the love seat.

"I *need* to make a phone call," she told him, her tone biting.

Melanie and Robbie must be nearly frantic with worry by now. What if it distracted them from their race preparation?

Then Julia wondered if the authorities would simply inform Melanie and Robbie she was in custody at Cadair Racing. If there was some kind of central database of prisoners, Melanie and Robbie could show up here any minute.

"I'm afraid I still can't allow a phone call," said Harrison.

"It's not that you can't," Julia retorted. "The problem is that you won't."

He gestured to the love seat. "We need to talk."

Once again, she wondered how much defiance she should show. She hated to give him his way. Then again, refusing to cooperate might simply slow down her release.

She sat, glancing at the food but not giving in to temptation on that front.

Harrison took one of the armchairs opposite.

"Starving yourself won't improve the situation," he pointed out.

"It'll give me emotional satisfaction," she told him honestly.

"In the short term, maybe. But if you're planning to fight or escape, or plot against me in any way, doesn't it make more sense to keep up your strength?"

It annoyed her that he was right. "You're expecting me to escape?"

He chuckled. "No. I'm expecting you to try."

Of course he didn't doubt he'd prevail. He was a member of the privileged class, after all.

"Well, I expected you to *quickly* discover that I am who I say I am, and let me go. Did you even check me out? Did you call *Equine Earth Magazine?*"

He leaned forward, lifted the silver coffeepot and poured two cups of the fragrant brew. "I looked them up on Google."

"Then you found out I'm me."

"I found out a woman named Julia Nash has written articles for them."

"That's *me*."

He added two lumps of sugar to one of the cups and pushed it her way. Then he lifted the other.

"What made you decide I took sugar?"

"You're young, you're American, you're a girl."

"That's ridiculous."

"*Do* you take sugar?"

She pursed her lips. "Yes."

"Then drink. Your keeling over doesn't help either of us."

She gave in. He was right on at least that count. She should keep up her strength. And the caffeine would help her stay alert, should an escape possibility present itself.

"If you'd give me back my purse, I can prove who I am," she said. "I have a driver's license."

"You also have a passport. Or rather, I have your passport."

"Then you *know* I'm Julia Nash."

He was obviously messing with her head for some obscure reason of his own. He had to have every intention of letting her go this morning. Hunger contracting her stomach, she reached for an almond-glazed Danish. If memory served, it was a long drive back to Dubai.

"Tell me again why you broke into Cadair Racing?" he asked.

Julia chewed then swallowed the first bite of the pastry, dabbing her lips with the white linen napkin. "As you've discovered for yourself, I'm a reporter for *Equine Earth Magazine*. I wanted to do a story on you and your horse."

"Which horse?"

"Millions to Spare."

"And what's your story angle?"

"His recent victories." That seemed generic enough.

"Why Millions to Spare? Ilithyia won more races this year."

Julia hesitated. This one was a little tougher.

Harrison raised his eyebrows.

She tried not to panic. She had to say something, anything. "Because of his…" No good. She drew a blank.

He gave her an extra few seconds, but then he shook his head.

"I was this close." He made a centimeter-size gap between his thumb and forefinger. "*This* close to believing you are who you say you are. But then you had to go and lie again."

"I'm not lying." She could easily do a story on him and Millions to Spare. Therefore, technically, she was telling the truth.

He reached into the inner pocket of his jacket. "I brought you your purse." He pushed it across the table.

Relief flooded through her. He *was* letting her go. She scooped up the ivory leather bag, snapped open the clasp and instantly noticed the deficiency. "My phone's not here." And neither was her passport, dashing her hopes that he might be setting her free.

Harrison stood. "Why would I give you back your phone?"

"So I can call a taxi."

He shook his head. "You're a criminal in my custody. You're not going anywhere until you tell me the truth."

Julia quickly looked through the purse, searching

for the other important item. Where was the cotton swab? Her heart beat deeply in her chest. Where was her DNA evidence?

Harrison started for the door. "We'll chat again after lunch."

"But—"

"Do enjoy your breakfast. Can I have Leila bring you anything else? A magazine perhaps."

Julia didn't want a magazine. She wanted a cell phone, a PDA, a walkie-talkie, anything with which to communicate with the outside world.

"Can I use a computer?" she tried.

He chuckled. "Right. That's likely."

"Well, can I at least get out of this room?" Communication devices were obviously not coming in, so she'd have to get out and find one.

He frowned as he considered her request.

She gestured to the fenced grounds below the balcony. There were also guards at the gate. Come to think of it, the place had an awful lot of security for a horse stable. Maybe horse thieves were common. Maybe Harrison had a legitimate reason to suspect she was trying to steal Millions to Spare.

"Where am I going to go?" she challenged him.

After another silent moment, he relented. "I'll have Leila show you to the main terrace. There's a pool there, and the staff will bring you anything you need."

Julia came to her feet, determined to push her luck as far as it could be pushed. "How about a tour?"

He raised one of his aristocratic brows. "A tour of what?"

"The palace, the gardens, the stable. If I'm going to do a story—"

He snorted his disbelief.

"—it'll be helpful to slot in some background."

He stared at her in silence.

"I *do* want to interview you."

He took a step toward her. "I'll give you a tour myself."

Okay, that wasn't exactly the perfect solution. She'd been hoping for Leila, or perhaps someone elderly, with hearing and sight challenges.

"Problem with that?" he asked.

"Not at all. I can interview you while we tour." At least it was a step in the right direction. She could always hope Harrison got called away or distracted while they were out, and then she'd seize the opportunity.

He opened the bedroom door and gestured for her to precede him. They followed the same route back to the great hall. From there, Harrison led her through the glass doors and onto a huge, concrete veranda. It overlooked a picturesque, tiled pool surrounded by palm trees and deck loungers, with a few umbrella tables in the distance.

As they stood side by side at the rail, Julia was struck again by the excesses of Harrison's lifestyle. Did he honestly feel the need to live like a king?

"What's your first question?" he asked.

"What on earth do you do for a living?" she asked without thinking.

He glanced quizzically down at her.

"You have a very, uh, nice place here," she elaborated.

"I own Cadair Racing," he told her.

"Right."

"Do you need a notebook for this?"

"No."

Again, that skeptical glance that told her he was onto her.

"I have a very good memory," she supplied, checking out the perimeter of the yard. The fence stretched into the ocean, but there was a chance she could wade around it.

"You rely on your memory?"

"Yes, I do."

He nodded. "Please proceed."

She wondered if the guards were armed. She hadn't thought about the possibility of getting shot.

"Julia?" Harrison prompted.

She blurted out the first question that came to her mind. "Your full name."

"The Right Honorable Lord Harrison William Arthur Beaumont-Rochester, Baron Welsmeire."

That got her attention. She squinted up at him. "You're joking."

"I'm quite serious."

So that's where he got all the money. "Are you in line for the British throne or something?"

"Number two hundred and forty-seven."

"You know the exact number?"

"Of course I know the exact number." His mouth twitched for a second in what had to be an aborted smile. "Two hundred and forty-six untimely deaths, and I'm in."

Julia struggled not to grin in return. "Will you kill them off yourself?"

His eyes squinted ever so suspiciously, reminding her that they were adversaries not friends. "Why? Is that what you'd do?"

The questions took her by surprise. "Hey, I might be willing to steal—" She cut herself off, astonished to realize she had been about to confess to stealing a swab of horse DNA.

"What?" he asked softly.

She frantically struggled to regroup.

"What is it you're willing to steal, Julia?"

Her brain scrambling, she blurted out the first thing that came to mind. "Toilet paper."

His brows went up.

"Back at the jail," she improvised. "I was getting pretty desperate."

He propped a hand against the concrete rail, his gray eyes narrowing. "Why don't I believe you?"

"Because you have trust issues."

He gave a dry chuckle, shaking his head. "Never had them before." Then he shook his head. "You are definitely a problem for me, Julia Nash."

She shrugged. "Then let me leave."

"I can't do that."

"Why not?"

He stared levelly at her for a few silent heartbeats, while the air all but crackled between them.

"If you know," he finally said, "then I don't need to tell you. And if you don't know, then I definitely can't tell you."

"That was more convoluted than your full name."

He gestured to a wide concrete staircase that led down to the pool and began walking. "Care for a swim?"

She kept pace with him. "I thought we were having a tour."

"It's getting warm."

"I'm fine."

He nodded, but he led her to one of the umbrella-covered tables and pulled out a chair.

Julia sighed. Getting a tour of the stables wasn't going to be as easy as she'd hoped.

They'd no sooner sat down than three servants arrived. One spread a tablecloth in front of them. One added silver, china and crystal place settings. While the third placed a floral arrangement, a plate of scones and jam, and a pitcher of peach-colored juice.

"Roughing it?" she asked him.

"Is that an interview question?" Harrison dismissed the servants and poured the juice himself.

"No." She sat back in her chair. "More of an editorial comment on your life."

"Am I about to get a lecture on privilege and excess?"

"You're number two hundred and forty-seven in line for the British throne. I'm guessing this isn't the worst of your excesses."

He put down the pitcher. "I see you remember the exact number."

"I told you I had a good memory."

"And here I thought your lack of a notebook meant you were lying through your teeth, and you never really intended to interview me at all."

Julia experienced a twinge of guilt. "Shows you how wrong you can be, doesn't it?"

"Say my name?"

"Harrison Rochester."

"You know what I mean."

Julia smiled to herself. "The Right Honorable Lord Harrison William Arthur Beaumont-Rochester." Then she paused for a beat. "Baron Welsmeire."

"Damn," he muttered, obviously surprised.

She pressed her advantage. "Has it occurred to you that I might not be lying?"

"Not even for a second."

Their gazes caught and smoldered, while some sort of arousal rose unwanted within her.

"Where were you born?" she finally asked him.

"This is going to be a bloody long interview."

She waited.

"I was born in Welsmeire Castle, south of Windermere—"

"You were born in a castle?"

"Yes."

"Why not a hospital?"

"Tradition. Bragging rights. I don't know."

"So your poor mother had you in a castle so you could brag about it in later life?"

He threw up his hands. "There *was* a doctor in attendance."

"Well, wasn't *that* good of you."

"I was a newborn at the time. Wait. No, not quite a newborn at the time."

"Barbaric," muttered Julia.

"It was her choice," said Harrison.

"Well, I'll be going to a hospital."

"Good to know."

Julia took a sip of her juice. "Brothers and sisters?"

"One sister. Elizabeth. Are you always this poorly prepared for an interview?"

Julia ignored his question. "So Elizabeth's on the British crown list, too?"

"Considerably farther down than me."

"Do you think that's fair?"

"Are you here to talk about my horse or revolution-ize the British monarchy?"

"We can't do both?"

He cracked a grin. "Better women than you have tried."

She moved a little closer. "Are you saying you agree with such a misogynistic approach to succession?"

He leaned in, as well. "I'm saying, at number two hundred and forty-seven, there's little I can do about it."

"You could oppose it."

"In my spare time? I'm a busy man, with a lot of important business dealings and connections, international connections."

Was he bragging?

He seemed to be watching for her reaction to that statement.

"Okay," she drawled. "And how long have you lived in Dubai?"

He straightened, peering at her a few seconds longer.

"I've owned Cadair for ten years. I spend winters here, summers in England."

"Are you married?"

"No."

"Engaged?"

He hesitated. "Not yet."

Julia experienced a jolt of curiosity. What kind of woman would marry a man like Harrison?

Then she quickly realized just about any kind of woman would marry him.

"Sounds like a scoop for me. Who is she?"

"Who says I've picked her out?"

Julia cocked her head. "So can I tell my female readers you're still available?"

"Julia, you have no female readers. You have no readers, period. This is a sham."

"Then why are you going along with me?"

"I'm trying to figure out what you're up to."

"If I leave, I can't be up to anything, can I?"

"If you leave," he countered, "you could be up to *absolutely* anything."

"I really need to call my friends."

He shook his head.

"They're going to think I'm dead."

He got that intense, probing look on his face again. "Now, why would they think that?"

"Because I disappeared for twenty-four hours in a foreign country. In my world, that's weird."

"And what world is that?"

She leaned forward, slowing her speech, enunciating each word. "Horse-race reporting."

"I almost believe you."

Chapter Four

It took Julia nearly two hours of feigned interest in libraries, paintings, statues, a wine cellar and Middle Eastern horticulture before Harrison was finally called away on business. He threatened to lock her back in her room, but she all but begged to see the stables. Finally, he relented, and left her in Leila's care.

It didn't take her long to figure out why he'd let her loose in the stables with a younger, smaller guard.

There wasn't a single phone to be found in the cavernous building. Julia had seen a lot of stables in her career, and this one was magnificent. A rubberized floor, cedar plank stalls and dozens of horses were illuminated by fluorescent lights embedded in the high, tin ceilings.

They passed a tack room, and she abruptly halted.

"Can I look in there?" she asked Leila.

"Yes, you can," said Leila politely, coming to a stop.

"Did you grow up in Dubai?" Julia asked, while she pretended to check out saddles and bridles and halters.

"I went to boarding school in Cambridge," Leila replied.

"Really?" That explained her perfect English and her rather mixed accent.

"I know you're looking for a phone," said Leila, regret in her dark-brown eyes.

"Harrison knows it, too," said Julia. "I'm guessing I won't find one here."

Leila shook her head.

"Yeah," said Julia with regret. "Otherwise he wouldn't have let me look around."

"Not without being here to watch you," said Leila. "His Lordship is quite intelligent."

"You actually call him that?"

"His Lordship?"

Julia nodded.

"That's his title."

"I've been calling him Harrison. Was I incredibly rude?"

Leila fought a smile.

"What?"

"You're his prisoner. Being rude seems like a small indiscretion."

Julia couldn't help but smile in return. "I suppose being rude is the least of my worries."

"He's a fair man," said Leila.

"Then why won't he let me make a phone call?"

Leila shrugged.

"You know, don't you?" asked Julia. "But you can't tell me. Out of loyalty to your employer."

Leila didn't answer.

"I can respect that," said Julia. "And I don't want you to get in trouble. But, I promise you, I wasn't trying to steal any horse."

Something flickered in Leila's expression.

"What?" asked Julia.

Leila shook her head.

"Damn. I'm sorry." She was putting the poor girl in an awkward position. "Can we carry on with the tour?"

Leila looked relieved.

They carried on down the barn hallway. Now that she knew there wasn't a phone to be found, Julia paid more attention to her second mission.

Millions to Spare.

Five hallways later, she spied the horse and abruptly stopped at the stall.

"You mind if I…" She flipped the latch and slipped inside before Leila could protest. "Don't worry," she called back. "I'm really good with horses."

That was a stretch. But since she'd survived a ride across the UAE cuddled up with Millions to Spare and his friends, she figured she was safe in his stall for a couple of minutes.

"I don't believe you should—"

"I'll just be a second. It's not like he has a phone," Julia joked.

She didn't have a cotton swab. But she'd seen enough crime dramas to know hair would work, too. Particularly if she got the roots.

Under the guise of petting the horse's neck, she plucked out a few hairs from his mane, tucking them into the pocket of her dress.

Leila's voice was worried. "Julia, really, you must—"

"On my way," Julia told Leila, slipping back out of the stall and latching the door. "He's a beautiful animal. I'm going to feature him in the article."

Leila gazed at her with what Julia could have sworn was disappointment.

"What?" Julia asked.

"Even I can tell you're lying."

Julia stopped. "I promise you, Leila. I'm not going to steal anything or hurt anybody."

Leila still looked skeptical.

Julia took a breath. "I have a friend who's in trouble," she said, being as honest as she could. "I'm here to find out more about Harrison and Millions to Spare. Nothing else."

The two women stared at each other for a long minute.

"Would you care to join me in the pool?" asked Leila.

Feeling the sweat trickle down her neck in the oppressive heat of the barn, Julia nodded to accept the invitation.

Harrison watched from a second-story window while Julia jackknifed from the diving board into the crystal-blue water of the estate's main pool. She wore a sleek, navy one-piece suit, her creamy skin flashing beneath the clear water.

She was an extremely attractive woman, lightly tanned, her body toned from some kind of an active life-style. Her auburn hair looked darker when it was wet, and he could imagine her deep-blue eyes flashing as she surfaced and called something to Leila.

Leila grinned as she shouted something back.

Harrison clenched his jaw.

Julia was down there co-opting Leila, gaining her trust. Which was exactly what a good operative would do.

There'd been a thousand signs that Julia wasn't a spy. She wasn't anywhere near alert enough to her surroundings. She didn't look around when she emerged from a doorway, didn't scan the distance or check for blind corners. She didn't even glance to see if any of his staff were concealing weapons, and she hadn't paid the slightest attention to his security guards while they toured the garden.

But then, just when he'd become convinced she was nothing more than a klutzy reporter, she'd raised his suspicions all over again.

Leila was vulnerable. She was young, impressionable. She'd be interested in someone from America. Julia had figured that out, and was obviously ready to exploit it.

"Your grandmother and Brittany are on the way from the airport." Alex joined Harrison at the window.

He followed the line of Harrison's gaze down to the pool. "So whatever it is you're going to do about Julia, you might want to do it in the next fifteen minutes."

"Why?"

"You being sarcastic?"

Harrison shook his head.

"Because, old man," Alex said with exaggerated patience. "Brittany may ask—oh, I don't know—something along the lines of, 'Harrison, who is that gorgeous woman swimming in your pool?' to which you would reply…?"

Harrison got Alex's point. "Right."

Alex clapped him on the shoulder. "If she's a spy, I'm a ballerina. Kick her loose, lock her up, send her back to the police station. But if you want a chance in hell with Brittany, get Julia out of the way."

"…and I need to see him *right* now," Nuri's voice roared from the hallway.

Harrison and Alex both pivoted toward the sound. They were halfway across the room when a breathless Nuri appeared in the doorway. "It's Millions to Spare."

"What about him?" Harrison demanded.

"He's been poisoned."

"*What?* How? Where's the vet?" Harrison elbowed his way past Nuri and into the hallway, striding for the main staircase.

Nuri immediately turned and kept pace, while Alex fell in behind them.

"The vet is attending the animal," said Nuri. "But, I am sorry to say…." His pause was coldly ominous. "It is too late."

"What do you mean, too late?" Harrison demanded, knowing full well what that had to mean. But his heart wasn't ready to accept that his horse was dead.

"He was found down, with tremors," said Nuri. "The vet came immediately, but the poor beast's heart and lungs gave out." The stable manager took a breath. "There were flecks of blood in his nostrils and his eyes had yellowed."

"Fannew?"

The tiny cactus grew wild all over the area, but the spines kept horses from eating them. Someone would have to have deliberately—

Julia.

Harrison hit the staircase and broke into a trot, marching through the great room and across the veranda.

A shriek of laughter came up from the pool.

He took the stairs two at a time, closing on poolside, where the two women were wrapped in towels beside one of the umbrella tables.

"Did she touch Millions to Spare?" he demanded of Leila.

Both women turned, and Leila's jaw dropped open at the sight of Harrison's expression.

"Did she touch Millions to Spare?" he repeated to another stunned silence from Leila.

"Yes," Julia cut in. "I was in his stall. Why—"

Without breaking his stride, Harrison grabbed her upper arm, pressing his other hand against her neck, and backed her into the wall of the pool house, his mind fogging red.

Her towel dropped, and she scrambled to keep her footing on the slippery deck.

Leila shrieked, and Alex shouted something unintelligible. But Harrison's rage was focused on Julia.

How had he been so stupid? Why had he trusted her out of his sight? Out of her locked room? For even one second?

"You killed my horse," he ground out.

Alex shouted his name again, but Harrison knew nobody would dare lift a finger to stop him.

Julia's jaw worked, her blue eyes wide in panic.

She couldn't speak, but she frantically shook her head.

"This is the Middle East," he told her, moving his face in close to hers, bombarding her with his rage. "Not America. I could kill you here and now."

"No," she rasped.

"Yes," he countered.

"I didn't—" She struggled to get the words out.

Yes, she did. She'd sneaked onto his land. She'd fixated on that horse from minute one. Then she'd sweet-talked her way into a tour of the barns.

"No!" It was Leila.

Her small hands dug at Harrison's back before somebody, certainly Nuri, dragged her away. But her actions jolted him back to some semblance of reality.

Leila was Nuri's daughter, and he'd surely punish her for intervening.

Harrison turned to look at the pair. "Leave her," he commanded.

Nuri's eyes narrowed.

"Have to talk to you," came Julia's hoarse voice.

Harrison turned back. Huge tears had formed in her eyes, magnifying her terror. She looked young and vulnerable, all but naked in the wet bathing suit.

He could have kicked himself.

What the *hell* was he doing?

This might be the UAE, but he was British, raised on the principle of justice, not revenge. There was no way in the world he'd kill somebody over a horse.

He loosened his grip.

"I didn't," she rasped again, her gaze going frantically around to Alex, Nuri, Leila and the other staff who had assembled.

"Please," she said to Harrison, those shimmering blue eyes getting to him. "I need to talk to you. Alone."

Harrison turned to Leila again, jerking his head to motion her forward.

The poor girl was shaking with terror.

"Thank you," Harrison said, making sure Nuri heard the words. "Now, can you tell me what she did?"

Leila was obviously incapable of speaking, so Harrison looked to her father. "She's a good girl," he told Nuri, a wealth of meaning in his tone.

Then he looked back down at Leila. "She went into the stall?"

Leila gave a shaky nod.

"Did she feed anything to Millions to Spare?"

"I don't… I don't think so."

"How long was she in there?"

"Two minutes, maybe."

Harrison nodded. Then he took in the assembled staff, selecting Darla. "Darla. Have Leila help you in the office for the rest of the day."

Darla quickly nodded and came forward for the girl. She would understand what Harrison wanted. He wasn't about to risk Nuri's wrath on Leila before the man had a chance to calm down.

Harrison turned back to Julia. "I'll have the whole truth, and I'll have it *right now*."

"Harrison?" came a puzzled, female voice.

All eyes turned to gape at a crisp and proper Brittany Livingston, standing frozen on the pool deck in ivory pumps, a knee-length, pleated, white skirt and a frosted pink, eyelet blouse with three-quarter-length sleeves. She stared at Harrison and Julia in obvious confusion.

Harrison immediately dropped his hand from Julia's throat, while Alex quickly intervened.

He positioned himself between Brittany and Harrison, blocking the woman's view.

"You must be Brittany," Alex put in smoothly, as if nothing out of the ordinary was going on. He offered his arm, deftly turning her back up the veranda stairs. "Please, introduce me to your grandmother. Harrison's tied up for just a short time."

Julia rubbed her chafed throat while Harrison

watched the woman named Brittany walk away with an American man. Julia was more stunned than hurt, but she was becoming very frightened.

Now that she knew she wasn't about to die, her mind grappled with the news that Millions to Spare was dead. Who could have done such a terrible thing?

"I need to talk to you," she began.

Harrison shot her a glare that shut her up. "You can bet your ass we're going to talk."

"Alone," she said. There was no reason not to tell him the whole truth now. But she didn't know what on earth could be going on, nor did she know who she could trust.

She didn't like the man named Nuri. He was the one who had had her arrested, and she was sure he would hurt Leila when he dragged her away from Harrison. She didn't trust him one little bit.

Harrison nodded his consent, steering her none too gently by the arm as he propelled her into a changing hut. He shut the door against the curious staff, then he leaned against it and crossed his arms over his chest in the dim, relatively cool building.

Julia wished she was wearing something more than a bathing suit. Her skin felt clammy, and he was watching every move she made.

She lowered herself onto a painted, wooden bench that wrapped around three sides of the octagonal hut.

"Start talking," said Harrison.

"I didn't kill Millions to Spare," she said. "I'd never, ever harm a horse."

"He was poisoned," Harrison said bluntly. "Fannew."

She had no idea what fannew might be, but horror

washed through Julia at the thought of the life leeching out of the poor, defenseless animal.

"I saw him at Nad Al Sheba," she began, determined to come clean. "He reminded me of a friend's horse, and I thought… That is, I hoped…" She didn't know how to explain it concisely.

"You looking to go back to jail?"

"He's the spitting image of Leopold's Legacy," she said.

"And who is Leopold's Legacy?"

"My friends, the Prestons—they're here to race Something to Talk About in the Sandstone Derby. But their champion stallion is Leopold's Legacy. There's a problem with his lineage, and he's been disqualified from the U.S. Stud Book, because they can't find his real sire."

She stood up, wrapping her arms around herself in a hug. "I wanted a DNA sample. I thought if I could either prove or disprove a relationship between the two horses, I could maybe…" She paused again. "Maybe help solve the mystery and get Leopold's Legacy reinstated."

"So you broke into my stable."

"I got trapped in the trailer."

"And you took a DNA sample?"

"Saliva."

"Without my permission."

She pushed back her slick, wet hair. "There was no point in upsetting you. The chances of disqualifying Millions to Spare were slim."

"At least he'd be alive."

"Do you honestly think I had anything to do with his death?"

Harrison rocked away from the door and took a step forward. "How would I know? All you've ever done since I met you is lie to me."

"I'm not lying."

He scoffed out a laugh, his emotionless gray eyes sending a chill through her damp body. "Now, where have I heard that before?"

She closed the space between them. "You have to listen to me," she said.

"No, *you* have to listen to *me*. I'm going to call the Prestons. I'm going to check out your latest story. And then maybe, just maybe, I won't send you back to jail."

A cold rush of fear snaked through Julia at the thought of that jail cell, and she gave an involuntary shiver.

"You have to take a blood sample," she told him. "Before they cremate Millions to Spare's body."

He shrugged out of his jacket. "You're not in a position to demand anything."

"I'm not demanding," she assured him.

He draped the jacket around her shoulders and paused.

"I'm asking," she whispered. "I lost the saliva sample, and then I took some hair from his mane, but I'm not sure…" She took a deep breath. "It would mean a lot to the Prestons."

"You know," said Harrison, something close to compassion flickering in his eyes. "This is the very first time your actions have actually matched your words."

She didn't know what to say to that.

He straightened the lapels of the jacket, and the backs of his knuckles briefly grazed her breasts. She was suddenly and sharply aware that they were alone, and she was barely dressed, and his word was law here.

"Finally," he said, voice husky.

"Finally what?" she asked nervously as an undeniable sizzle of attraction filled the air.

"Finally, you're being honest with me."

A moment of taut silence stretched between them. He shifted almost imperceptibly toward her, his eyes clearly telegraphing his intent.

"Don't get the idea that I'm easy," she quickly warned him.

"Because you wear a thong?"

"A gentleman would forget about that."

He shifted closer still, tugging ever so slightly on the lapels of his jacket. But, surprisingly, she wasn't afraid. There was no anger in his expression, more curiosity than anything.

"Whatever gave you the idea I was a gentleman?"

"You're the Right Honorable Lord Harrison William Arthur Beaumont-Rochester."

His gaze fixed on her lips, eyes darkening with obvious desire. "That only means I'm from a long line of reprobates and libertines."

"Nothing good can come of you kissing me," she pointed out, even though it was starting to seem like a very interesting idea.

"So far, nothing good has come from me meeting you."

"So cut your losses."

She could almost see the debate going on inside his head. It lasted several minutes. And by the time he eased back, her pulse was racing and her skin was prickling.

He dropped his hands and nodded to his jacket. "There's a phone inside the pocket."

Seconds after that, he'd walked out, leaving Julia alone, sunlight streaming through the open door.

Harrison quietly entered the palace through a side door, heading directly into a small study and sitting down at the computer. He brought up an article on Leopold's Legacy and quickly scanned it through. By the end, his worry over Julia and the secretary-general's reception was replaced by a new fear for Cadair Racing.

Leopold's Legacy's sire had originally been listed as Apollo's Ice. Apollo's Ice was also Millions to Spare's sire.

The odds were overwhelming that Millions to Spare's death was linked to the Leopold's Legacy mystery. Which meant it was somehow linked to Julia. Which meant he needed to talk to the Prestons, and he needed to talk to them as soon as possible.

He asked the first staff member he came across to have the vet meet him in his study, to please invite Julia to dry off and meet them there, too, and to bring him all the information available on the Prestons and Leopold's Legacy.

Finally, he forced a relaxed, cheerful expression onto his face and veered into the great hall, where Alex would have taken Brittany.

"Grandmother," he greeted, crossing to where she sat on a French provincial chair overlooking the east garden. He held out both hands to Lady Hannah Beaumont-Rochester.

As always, his grandmother was perfectly groomed, every blond hair in place, tasteful earrings at her ears. She was wearing a shimmering, brown-and-gold-leaf-patterned blouse paired with a plain, brown skirt.

She smiled warmly, reaching out to touch him. "Harrison. So good to see you, dear."

He leaned forward for a quick hug and cheek kiss.

"How was your flight?" he asked her.

"Very nice. But, my, it is hot here today."

"Shall I have the air-conditioning adjusted?"

"It's fine inside." Her gaze shifted to Brittany, who had stood up from her chair.

"Brittany," Harrison greeted, holding out both hands to her, and drawing her in for a slightly more personal hug.

Then he drew back to look into her smiling face. Like his grandmother, everything about Brittany was perfect. From her pale pink-and-white outfit to her jewelry, her hair. She was stunningly beautiful, always had been.

Harrison was ten years her senior, and he could remember every stage of her growing up. No awkward teenage years for Brittany; she'd always been poised and attractive.

"I explained about the accident," Alex put in.

Harrison shifted his attention to Alex, looking for clues on the story he'd come up with.

"That poor girl," said Grandmother.

"A close call," said Alex, and Harrison waited to understand.

"Harrison had to haul her out of the pool," Alex continued. "At first, we thought mouth-to-mouth might be necessary. But a few firm backslaps did the trick."

"Right." Harrison nodded. It was lame as stories went, but he supposed it was better than admitting he'd been about to strangle Julia.

He looked at Brittany, and he couldn't help but contrast her crisp appearance to Julia's disheveled state.

Brittany inspired respect. Julia, well, Julia had inspired something completely different.

He gave his head a quick shake to banish the image. "Please, may I offer you lunch?" He gestured to the hallway that would take them to several informal dining areas.

His grandmother came slowly to her feet.

Alex moved to help her, but Harrison gave him a quick shake of the head. Lady Beaumont-Rochester did not yet take kindly to assistance.

"Please," she said. "Not outside in the heat."

"We have a lovely dining room overlooking the fountains," said Harrison. He gallantly held out an arm to his grandmother.

Alex stepped in next to Brittany.

"I'm afraid I can't join you for lunch," Harrison said in a voice loud enough that they could all hear it. "Some last-minute preparations for the party tomorrow night, and a few other business details. I hope you don't mind."

"You men and your business," said Grandmother. But Harrison knew it would take a whole lot more than an inconvenient business meeting to upset her today. She'd be thrilled by his invitation to Brittany. He could probably do no wrong in her eyes for quite a while to come.

"Of course we don't mind," Brittany put in.

"I'm sure Alex would be happy to join you," Harrison offered.

"My pleasure," said Alex in a carefully neutral voice.

Harrison was sure he was the only one who realized Alex was ticked off. Alex didn't want to entertain the ladies over lunch. He wanted to find out what the hell was going on with Millions to Spare and Julia.

Chapter Five

Brittany Livingston didn't like being humored, and she certainly didn't like being lied to, and Mr. Alex Lindley had been doing both for the past hour. That woman at the pool hadn't been drowning. Harrison was clearly reaming her out. Which meant she must have done something pretty terrible, because Brittany had known Harrison her entire life, and she'd never seen him anywhere near that angry.

And something was still going on.

Alex Lindley had glanced at his watch at least three times since they'd finished lunch and Lady Hannah had excused herself for a nap.

"If there's somewhere you have to be," Brittany offered, her tone a study in civility.

"Nowhere important," said Alex, though the strain around his mouth told her differently.

It was on the tip of her tongue to probe for answers.

Where was Harrison? Who was the mysterious woman? What kind of party disaster would take him away from his duties as host?

Lady Hannah had been pushing Harrison to propose to Brittany for years. She'd made no secret of the fact she thought they were a good match. And she'd clearly taken this invitation as a signal that he was ready to commit.

Brittany had to admit, she was completely open to a signal from Harrison. He was a fine man. He'd make a good husband and a terrific father.

The list of men acceptable to Brittany's own father was relatively short. Not that Brittany couldn't have defied her father and married whomever she wanted. But, honestly, she'd never met a man remotely worth the trouble of being shunned and disinherited.

But if Harrison's invitation truly was a signal, then his behavior since she'd arrived was bizarre. And Alex's lame excuses and prattling conversation were more than frustrating.

"Would you care for a stroll in the gardens?" asked Alex in a slightly strained voice.

She gazed at him, biting her tongue against questions about his role at Cadair.

He seemed out of place in the elegant dining alcove, as if the room could barely contain his raw energy. His hands were fisted on his knees. He had a rakish chin with an interesting little scar on the left side. He was tall and muscular with worldly brown eyes and a shock of dark hair that whisked across his forehead.

"Why do I get the feeling that's not a question you ask a lot of women?" she dared.

His dark eyes narrowed in confusion.

"Are you truly a stroll-in-the-gardens kind of man?"

"I don't know what you're—"

"You have somewhere you want to be, true?"

He didn't answer, but there was something about his smoldering expression that allowed her to drop social convention.

"And it has something to do with the woman by the pool?"

Still nothing. But his eyes darkened further.

Brittany waded determinedly into the silence. "Please don't let me keep you." No sense in both of them being frustrated.

"I'm at your service, ma'am." The polite words were somewhat compromised by his tight jaw.

Brittany decided to throw all caution to the wind. "Who is she?"

"A walk?" he offered again. "The garden?"

But now that she'd started down this road, she didn't want to back off. "Then, who are you?"

"I'm the senior vice president of Cadair International."

That surprised her. She didn't know what she'd expected. A bodyguard, maybe? "Funny we haven't met before."

"I don't attend many social functions."

"Ah." She sat forward, liking that his facade had cracked. "Was that a slight?"

"No, ma'am. Of course not."

"Are you suggesting social functions are the only places you'd find me?" It was probably true. But there were days Brittany wished it weren't.

He stared at her in silence. There was something

dangerous in his eyes, and she found it intrigued her. Men never looked at her that way. Most of them were too afraid of her father.

"Can we please," he finally said on an exasperated sigh, "for the love of God, go for a walk in the garden?"

"If you tell me who she is."

"She's Julia Nash. A reporter for *Equine Earth Magazine*."

Brittany rocked back. That wasn't what she'd expected. Not that she'd expected anything in particular. "She must have written some story."

Alex rose. "I don't know what you mean."

"I mean," said Brittany, coming to her feet, "the woman wasn't drowning."

"You really need to talk to Harrison about this."

"Why? Don't you make up all his lies for him?"

Alex's jaw went tight all over again. "Does Harrison know you're like this?"

Brittany couldn't help but grin. She wasn't normally like this. But there was something about Alex that brought out the devil in her. "You mean nosy?"

"I mean rude and sarcastic."

She gave him her sweetest, most innocent, wide-eyed, finishing-school smile. "But, Alex. I'm never rude and sarcastic. Ask anyone." She turned for the door with a flourish.

Julia clutched the door handle of the SUV as Harrison rounded a bend on the dirt road leading to Route Eleven. They were meeting Melanie and Robbie in Dubai this afternoon, an hour's drive away.

"Melanie said they'd checked the hospitals," Julia told Harrison, recapping her telephone conversation.

"And they called the police. But the police didn't know anything about me."

"That's because my bribe was large enough to erase all records of your arrest."

Julia's attention shot from the dusty road to Harrison's profile. "Your bribe?"

He nodded, wrestling the steering wheel as they rounded another bend.

"You bribed the police to release me?"

He gave her a brief sideways glance. "You'd rather I'd left you there?"

"What kind of man are you?"

"Oh, right. You break into my property. You lie through your little teeth. You try to steal from me. And *my* ethics are in question?"

"I wouldn't even know how to bribe a police officer." She didn't mean for the assertion to sound superior, but somehow it did.

He hit the brakes as a herd of camels appeared, ambling alongside the road. "I find cash usually works best."

It was unnerving to discover he did this with some regularity. "So I was never really in your custody?"

"Yes, you were."

"But not legally."

"I don't know if you want to hang your hat on the term *legally* under these circumstances."

"Who *are* you?"

"The Right Honorable Lord Harrison William Arthur Beaumont-Rochester, Baron Welsmeire."

"Did you bribe somebody to get the title, too?"

"For God's sake. It was a minor charge. I helped a couple of officers with their pension funds to expedite its dismissal. A thank-you wouldn't be out of order."

The road turned from dirt to pavement, and a few adobelike houses and some scattered greenery popped up along the desert.

"Thank you," said Julia, reminding herself how grateful she'd been to him that night.

He grunted a response, pressing down on the accelerator as the road smoothed out and traffic began to increase.

"Do you always drive this fast?"

"In case you hadn't noticed, I have company back at Cadair."

"Who was she?" asked Julia.

"My grandmother."

"She sure didn't look like your grandmother." In fact, the woman looked like a movie star—perfect nose, perfect teeth, perfect hair.

"Brittany's not my grandmother. She's a family friend from London."

"A close friend?" asked Julia with obvious meaning.

Harrison sighed. "Yes. A close friend."

"Oh." So much for pursuing anything resembling Stockholm syndrome. Not that Julia had planned to pursue it. But that almost kiss had been, well, almost amazing.

She supposed Brittany was the reason he'd backed off.

Poor Brittany.

Harrison wasn't much of a prize if he'd seriously considered kissing another woman only moments after his girlfriend had arrived from London.

"So that's what you meant by 'not yet.'"

Harrison glanced her way, raising his brows.

"When I asked you if you were engaged, you said 'not yet.'"

"And I'm not."

"But Brittany's on the short list."

"Brittany is the short list."

"Yet…" Julia bit down on her bottom lip. None of her business.

"I didn't kiss you," said Harrison, catching her meaning as he geared down, slowing his speed and easing into a traffic circle.

"But you thought about—"

"Brittany and I have an understanding."

"That you kiss other women?"

"Not that kind of an understanding."

Julia thought about it. "Oh, my," she said, getting the point. "You're royalty. Is she royalty, too? I didn't think they did arranged marriages anymore."

"It's not an arranged marriage."

"Right. It's an *understanding*. Aren't you worried your children might have webbed toes?"

"I can't believe you said that."

Julia couldn't actually believe she had, either. Maybe it was a backlash from having been under his control for two days. And now that it was over, she was free to speak her mind.

Still, it was rude and uncalled-for. It was none of her business who Harrison did or did not marry. Another couple of hours, and she'd be out of his life forever. And Brittany was probably a perfectly wonderful woman. They'd certainly make gorgeous children together.

"Did you find out how to ship Millions to Spare's blood sample?" she asked.

Harrison nodded, apparently as eager as she was to get out of their previous conversation. "My vet's in contact with Carter Phillips. They're going to run the test in Switzerland to save time."

Julia nodded, sobering. "I can't decide whether to hope it's nothing, or hope it's something."

"It's not nothing," said Harrison.

The road widened to four lanes, and Harrison moved to pass the panel truck in front of him.

Julia waited.

"Apollo's Ice is Millions to Spare's sire," he said.

Julia digested that news. "Picture of Perfection, the horse Carter found in California, was also sired by Apollo's Ice."

"I'm sure Carter will warn them," said Harrison.

"It's his fiancée's horse," said Julia. "And maybe the poisoning had nothing to do with the mystery of Leopold's sire."

"Possibly," Harrison allowed.

"I can't figure out what would be gained by killing Millions to Spare."

"It could be as simple as revenge."

"Against you?" she asked.

"First place I'd be looking is my enemies or rival stables."

It seemed far-fetched that a rival stable would go so far as to kill an innocent animal. But millions of dollars were at stake. And the rich were involved. Who knew where the trail would lead?

Then, an idea came to Julia.

She paused, taking in Harrison's profile, screwing up her courage.

"Would you mind if I wrote the story?"

He glanced at her.

"About Millions to Spare? I could help with the investigation, then write a story exposing the killer."

"You want to turn his death into a salacious headline?"

"I want to turn it into a serious news story. Somebody killed a valuable Thoroughbred, and there has to be a reason why."

"And you want the byline."

"Yes," Julia admitted. "I want the byline."

"There you go again," said Harrison as he pulled past another truck.

"What?"

"Making your actions match your words."

"Is that a yes?"

"We'll see."

She opened her mouth to argue, but then decided to leave well enough alone. She'd planted the seed of the idea, and he hadn't said no. She'd have to be happy with that for the moment.

Melanie pulled Julia firmly into her arms in their hotel suite at Jumeirah Beach, holding tight and rocking back and forth. "I am *so* happy to see you."

"It was a big mix-up," said Julia, deciding to downplay her time at Harrison's.

Melanie drew back. "We're just glad you're safe."

"I'm safe. How's Something to Talk About?"

"He's fine," said Robbie, giving Julia a quick hug himself. It was the first one she could remember from him. When he released her, she was surprised by the joy and relief on his face.

She stepped in with the introductions. "Robbie, Melanie, this is Harrison. He's…" She hesitated. Her rescuer? Her kidnapper?

"The owner of Cadair Racing," Harrison put in.

Robbie stuck out his hand, and the men shook. "Pleasure to meet you."

"Me, too," said Melanie, offering her own hand. "I was very sorry to hear about your stallion."

Harrison nodded. "Thank you. Any news from America?"

"I wish there was," said Robbie. "We're holding out hope. If we can identify Legacy's real sire, and if he's registered, the problems could all go away. Since Apollo's Ice was the listed sire, we're *very* interested in Millions to Spare."

Harrison nodded. "Can you bring me up to speed?"

Robbie gestured to the table where his laptop was set up, and the two men settled into chairs.

Melanie pulled Julia down on the sofa. "You were in *jail?*"

Julia shuddered. "Thankfully, not for long. They let me go home with Harrison last night."

"Tell me again why he wouldn't let you call us?"

"He seemed to think I had accomplices. I didn't want to tell him about the DNA, so my story kept falling apart."

Melanie reached out to rub Julia's arm. "Talk about above and beyond the call of duty."

"I just wish I'd found something more."

"We have one more DNA sample."

Julia nodded. At least that was something.

Robbie and Harrison rose from the table.

"Thank you for bringing Julia back," said Robbie.

Harrison shot an amused look Julia's way. "You might want to tell her she should stick to reporting."

"I *was* reporting," Julia felt compelled to point out.

"Her story on us will be a lot safer," said Melanie.

"Perfect," said Harrison. "She can stick with her strengths."

Julia glared at him. She wasn't some hothouse flower who couldn't handle the serious stuff. Heck, she'd survived prison. And she'd survived his temper.

"I'm still doing the Millions to Spare story," she warned.

"Is that a question or a decree?"

There was something in his stance that gave her pause. She knew he wasn't a man to mess with, but she also knew he'd mow her down like ripe alfalfa if she gave him half a chance.

"I'd appreciate your cooperation," she finally said.

There was a telltale glint in his eye that told Julia he'd taken her words as capitulation. They weren't. She was definitely doing the story. She was simply being polite about it.

Melanie glanced curiously back and forth between them.

"I'll be at the Sandstone Derby tomorrow," Harrison said to Robbie. "Hopefully we'll have some answers from Switzerland by then."

His gaze paused on Julia, giving her a chance to add something, but she couldn't for the life of her figure out what that might be. It seemed silly to stay angry but ridiculous to thank him.

"I'll see you again tomorrow," he told all three of them.

Robbie walked him to the suite door.

There was nothing more to be done prior to the test results.

"Is Something to Talk About ready to race?" asked Julia. No matter what happened with Millions to Spare and Leopold's Legacy, Melanie's and Robbie's heads had to be in the race tomorrow.

"He's ready," said Robbie.

"I worked with him this morning," said Melanie. "He's learning the race ramp-up routine." She smiled like a proud parent. "He knows tomorrow is the day."

"If I grab my notebook," asked Julia, "can I get a few quotes from you now? If his finish is strong, I'm going to want to file the story as soon as the race is over. I'm sure *Equine Earth* would put some excerpts into a daily for us."

In Harrison's opinion, there was nothing like a parade to the post. His two-year-old Zetwinkler, along with the Prestons' Something to Talk About, twitched and frisked their way to the starting gates for the featured running of the Sandstone Derby. The horses' sleek coats gleamed, and the jockeys' colors flashed bright under the racetrack lights.

From his suite above the Maktoum grandstands, Harrison could see the crowd coming to its feet, while those on the lawns surged forward to the fence. The announcer's voice grew more excited, switching languages, earning cheers from the crowd as favorite horses were announced.

Next to him, Brittany straightened in her chair and leaned toward the window. His grandmother raised her binoculars, taking a bead down the track.

Then the bell rang, and sixteen gates clanged open as the announcer began calling the race.

Zetwinkler was off to a good start, pulling up the center, near the middle of the pack. Harrison kept his eye on the Cadair colors. A length and a half off the leader, Zetwinkler was holding strong, moving into fifth, then fourth, and chasing down the Japanese horse for third.

Harrison also caught sight of Something to Talk About. Far on the outside, the horse was lagging behind for the rest of the backstretch.

Then, suddenly, he seemed to gather his strength. At the nine-hundred-meter mark, he drove his way up, closing the gap on the leaders. Harrison watched Melanie glance around, keeping herself oriented, staying outside the pack, making sure she had room.

Meanwhile, Zetwinkler was closing in on the leader himself. Harrison stood up, as did Brittany and even his grandmother, while Zetwinkler pulled ahead by a neck.

Then, around the turn, Melanie closed in. Something to Talk About held his pace, pushing though third, then second. Then he was neck and neck with Zetwinkler, and the two horses burst from the pack, battling it out.

At three hundred meters, headed for home, Harrison silently pulled for his own horse, but could sense Something to Talk About's passion.

Sure enough, at two hundred meters, Something to Talk About grabbed a whole new gear. He streaked clear of Zetwinkler, driving his way past the grandstands to the roar of the crowd, through the finish line, claiming the Sandstone Derby championship.

Melanie stood in her stirrups as the horse slowed its pace.

"Too bad," said Brittany, placing her hand on Harrison's arm.

He patted her hand, grinning ear to ear. "That is one fine animal."

She glanced quizzically up at him. "It took second."

"I meant Something to Talk About."

"Oh."

He smiled down at her. "I spoke with Melanie Preston yesterday. This is a big win for her."

Brittany nodded and gave him a lovely smile. "That's very generous of you."

"There'll be other races," he told her.

Grandmother lowered her binoculars. "That was magnificent," she beamed, taking note of Harrison's hand over Brittany's, her smile growing even wider.

"Shall we join them in the winner's circle?" asked Harrison.

"You young people go and enjoy yourselves," said Grandmother. "I'm a bit too tired for a party tonight."

Harrison would rather talk with Julia, Melanie and Robbie in person, but he wouldn't force his grandmother to stay up late. "We can all head back," he offered.

"Nonsense," she told him, and her expression gave away her matchmaking ploy.

"Shall I call you a car?" Harrison asked, testing his theory.

"What a lovely idea."

He extracted his cell phone, dialing his regular car service, happy to go along with his grandmother's machinations.

After settling her for the ride back to Cadair, Harrison escorted Brittany to the winner's circle. They arrived just in time to see Something to Talk About draped in flowers and Melanie hoist the trophy.

Beaming with pride, Robbie was at the horse's head for pictures.

Julia was talking to one of the photographers, and Harrison caught her eye.

She smiled at him, then finished the conversation before approaching.

"Brittany," Harrison began, "this is Julia Nash."

Julia gave Brittany a polite greeting.

"Did you see the race?" she asked Harrison.

"My horse came second," he replied.

"Zetwinkler is Cadair?" She jotted down a note. "I should have paid more attention to the colors. Of course, he'll be featured in my article. It was a great race," she breathed.

"That it was," said Harrison, taking in her sleeveless, little navy dress, her utilitarian shoulder bag and disheveled hair, along with her spiral notepad and the pen in her hand.

She was in stark contrast to Brittany, whose blond hair was immaculate, and whose tiny, beaded evening bag matched her mint-green cocktail dress and the sheer scarf she'd draped across her shoulders. Brittany's shoes were more stylish, as well. Julia sported lower heels with plain leather straps.

It should have been no contest, but there was something in the animation of Julia's expression that engaged Harrison.

"Can I get a quote from you for the article?" she asked.

He glanced at Brittany, feeling unaccountably guilty, even though he hadn't done a thing wrong.

"Perhaps I'll sit down and have some tea." Brittany pointed to a group of open-air tables nearby.

"I won't keep him long," Julia promised.

"You sure you don't mind?" he asked Brittany.

"It's no trouble at all." She turned away.

Grateful that Brittany was so patient and even tempered, Harrison turned his attention to the interview. "Go ahead," he told Julia.

She raised her pen. "What did you think of the finish?"

He drew a breath. "It was magnificent. Two up-and-coming stallions battling it out in the homestretch. It doesn't get more exciting than that."

"Were you surprised to see Something to Talk About pull away?"

"Something to Talk About is clearly a well-bred, well-trained and enthusiastic racer." Then he leaned in. "Is that the kind of thing you need?"

She grinned up at him, a glint in her eye that caused a hitch in his chest. It was an annoying and unwanted reaction.

Then again, she was undeniably an attractive woman. And he was a healthy man. He'd get over it. He always did.

"Could you work in something about respecting the Prestons?" she asked.

"Write whatever you want. You can attribute it to me."

"Thanks." She jotted down a couple more notes while his cell phone rang.

"Hello?"

"Harrison?"

Harrison recognized the American voice, and touched Julia's arm to get her attention. "Yes?"

"This is Carter Phillips. I've just spoken with the lab tech in Switzerland. Millions to Spare is, was, a half brother to Leopold's Legacy."

"Not a half brother to Picture of Perfection?"

"Definitely not."

Harrison was not only surprised by the information, he was unnerved. This meant there was no way the mistake in Leopold's Legacy's breeding was accidental. And the death of Millions to Spare had to be related.

It put the mystery in a whole new realm.

"Whoever secretly sired Leopold's Legacy also secretly sired your stallion," said Carter. "DNA doesn't lie."

He was right about that. Which left a million unanswered questions.

"Can we keep this under wraps?" asked Harrison, as Julia's expression grew curious.

"Absolutely," said Carter Phillips. "We'll continue our research at this end."

"And I'll investigate the poisoning before the trail gets cold."

"Thanks," said Carter.

"Thank you," said Harrison, ending the call.

"What is it?" Julia hissed.

"They're half brothers," he told her.

"Millions to Spare and Picture of Perfection?"

"Millions to Spare and Leopold's Legacy."

Julia's eyes widened. "How can that be?"

"I have no idea."

Chapter Six

Julia had to practically run to catch up to Harrison as he crossed the winner's circle. Her mind was scrambling over the DNA revelation. They had a serious clue here. And she might have a very serious story.

Harrison smiled broadly and held out his hand to Robbie. "Congratulations to Quest Stables."

"Thank you," Robbie responded, and Melanie waved to them from atop the horse.

Harrison casually reeled Robbie in, his tone going lower, but Julia could still make out the words. "I don't mean to sound all cloak-and-dagger," he said, "but keep smiling and pretend I'm congratulating you."

Robbie smiled, and Julia smiled along with them.

"Millions to Spare and Leopold's Legacy have the same sire. I don't know who's watching us together, so

I'm going to back off now and walk away. You call Carter Phillips for the details."

Robbie nodded, clapping a hand on Harrison's shoulder. "Thank you very much," he said, sincerity in his eyes.

Harrison gave a sharp nod and turned away.

Julia quickly fell into step beside him.

"That goes for you, too," he growled down at her. "You need to stay away from me and go back to America."

"I can help you investigate."

He gave a snort of disbelief. "You couldn't get a DNA swab without getting thrown in jail."

While that might be true, she had a right to this story. She wanted to help the Prestons. She wanted to expose Millions to Spare's killer. "I'll stay out of your way," she promised.

"That seems unlikely."

"I want the story, Harrison."

He stopped. "Julia, somebody out there was willing to kill my horse over all of this."

"Maybe I can figure out who?"

"Go back to America."

"But—"

"Seriously, Julia. Go home. I'll call you right away if we find anything." Then he stepped back. "Goodbye."

A look passed between them, and she could have sworn it was longing. But he quickly turned away.

And then he was gone, and Melanie was beside her.

"How bizarre is that?" asked Melanie.

"Pretty bizarre," said Julia.

Harrison sat down next to Brittany, and Julia found she couldn't watch them together.

She forced herself to concentrate on the crowds and the horses and jubilant shouts instead. She nudged Melanie in the shoulder. "You won."

Melanie beamed. "I did."

Juggling her bag, her pen and her notebook out of the way, Julia pulled Melanie in for a hug. "You actually won. It was fabulous. And Harrison gave me a quote. And I'm going to file this article. If we're lucky, some of the daily newspapers will pick it up."

The smile faded from Melanie's face. "What do you think is going on? How did a horse end up dead?"

Julia shook her head. "I have no idea. But I'm going to stay behind and find out."

Melanie's expression registered surprise. "You're staying in Dubai?"

"I am. The clues are here."

Harrison might object, but it wasn't Harrison's decision to make.

Melanie hesitated. "Are you sure it's safe?"

"The only person causing me any grief was Harrison. I think he's over that now."

Melanie gave a slow, considered nod. "Then keep the hotel room. Quest will pay."

"I can't do that."

"Robbie and I have to travel with Something to Talk About. You'll be helping the family out by staying here."

"I'm also doing it for the story." Julia wanted to be honest.

"I know you are." Melanie squeezed Julia's shoulders. "You deserve the story. Now, I have to head for the barns. The last thing we want to do is mess with Something to Talk About's schedule."

"He was a good boy today," said Julia.

"He was a very good boy. My brother is over the moon."

The following evening, it was easy for Harrison to see that Brittany was the consummate hostess.

It was four o'clock, and a few of the out-of-town guests were arriving early to the party. She cheerfully and easily greeted princes, generals and captains of industry. She laughed and chatted in several languages, introducing one guest to the other while keeping half an eye on the servers to make sure none of the guests were neglected.

Alex appeared at Harrison's elbow. "The pipeline meeting is set for five o'clock."

"Good." Harrison kept his eyes on Brittany.

Alex was silent for a moment.

"So she's the one?" he asked.

"She's the one," Harrison confirmed, more convinced than ever.

"Hmm." There was something in Alex's tone.

"What?"

"I'm not so sure."

"What's not to be sure? She's perfect."

"You think?"

Now what the hell did that mean?

Alex reacted to Harrison's astonishment. "There seems to be an edge to her."

"An edge? To Brittany?"

"Sarcasm, hostility."

Harrison snorted in disbelief. "What have you been drinking? Look at her."

"She does present well," said Alex.

"I do believe you're jealous."

"Not."

"Come to think of it, get your leering eyes off my future fiancée."

"Believe me, Harrison. I haven't the slightest attraction to your future fiancée."

"Now I know you're lying. Check out her eyes, her hair. Or look at those legs—long, toned, straight."

"Are you talking about a wife or a broodmare?"

With a start, Harrison realized he *had* been thinking of her perfection as a mother, rather than imagining those straight legs wrapped around him.

It had to be his innate respect for her. That was the only explanation.

Then his mind involuntarily flashed to Julia. Seeing her in that bathing suit that left so little to the imagination, he could easily picture her legs wrapped around his waist. And when he conjured up that particular image, he didn't feel respectful at all. He felt…

"Let's get a drink," he said to Alex.

Sitting in the back of a taxi as it pulled up to the Jumeirah Beach Hotel, Julia caught sight of Pamjeet the doorman trotting up to meet them.

There was something lurking in his dark eyes, and a funny feeling tripped along her spine.

They'd barely stopped, when he opened the back door, blocking her way out, leaning in to talk to her.

"You must not come in to the hotel," he said in an earnest low tone, close to her ear.

"What—"

"Go now. The police were here."

Everything inside Julia stilled as her memory flashed to the dismal jail conditions.

"What do I—"

"Do you have your passport?" He kept his voice low so the driver wouldn't overhear.

She nodded. "Yes."

"The airport," he called to the driver, drawing back.

"Now?" Julia's frightened eyes met Pamjeet's.

He gave her a nod and slammed the door, turning back to his duties as if nothing untoward had happened.

The taxi pulled into traffic and sped toward the airport in the waning daylight.

Julia tried to wrap her head around what she'd just heard. The police were looking for her? Harrison's bribe must not have worked as well as he'd thought.

She strained to see out the back window, checking for signs of pursuit. There was nothing but regular downtown traffic—sedans, delivery trucks and the occasional limousine.

Her luggage was still in the hotel room. She couldn't really afford to replace all those clothes, not to mention her small jewelry collection. Still, anything was better than going back to jail.

She watched the skyscrapers whiz by as the driver expertly navigated his way through intersections and traffic circles on the way to the airport. She'd switched her plane ticket to the middle of next week. Would they let her change back? Would they have any available seats?

She could get on the first plane to anywhere, she supposed. What did it matter which route she took home? And what did it matter how long it took her to pay off the credit-card bill? The only thing that mattered was that she get out of the country.

After long, tense minutes in traffic, she breathed a sigh of relief as the planes and lighted hangars of the airport came into view next to the wide, divided highway. They were almost there.

"What time is your flight, ma'am?" came the driver's voice.

"I don't know. I'm not sure."

He nodded. "There seems to be a traffic delay. I hope it will not inconvenience you."

She shifted to the middle of the backseat, sitting straight to look out the windshield at the main terminal building. So close, yet so far away.

"Can you tell what it is?"

He nodded to the road ahead. "A roadblock."

"An accident?"

"I don't believe so, ma'am. It's a checkpoint. The police."

"Is this common?"

"Not common."

Uh-oh. "What are they checking for?"

"I do not know."

It couldn't be.

But her pulse started to pound in agitation.

She was running from the police, and they had a roadblock at the airport? Coincidence?

She tried to calm herself down. There was no way they'd call out the SWAT team for attempted horse theft. The mere thought was ridiculous. She was letting herself get freaked out over nothing.

She forced herself to sit back, swiping the beads of sweat from her forehead.

They'd be through the roadblock in a few minutes.

She'd buy a ticket to, well, anywhere. And she'd be on her way out of UAE.

"Do you have your passport, ma'am?"

"Why?"

"The police will require identification."

Julia's heartbeat thickened. She inhaled, and she could swear she smelled the stale, gray dress from the prison. She saw the wriggling centipede, felt the sharp pressure on her bladder.

"Turn around," she said to the driver.

"Pardon me, ma'am?"

"I..." She pretended to paw through her purse. "I forgot something. I need to go back."

"To the hotel."

"No! Not the hotel." *Think, think, think.* Would the embassy help her? Could they help her? She didn't dare risk it. "To Cadair Racing. It's north, on Route Eleven. Past Ajman."

"As you wish, ma'am."

The driver signaled and painstakingly moved one lane to the right. But there he was trapped by a panel truck.

Julia trained her eyes on the road ahead, praying for some kind of exit.

There it was.

The driver jockeyed back and forth, trying to get around the truck in the snail-paced traffic.

She glanced at the flashing lights on the looming roadblock. She clenched her jaw, clenched her fists, willed a spot to open up in the right-hand lane.

Her driver signaled, and inched, and honked and nudged.

When he successfully switched to the exit lane, she could have shouted for joy.

* * *

Brittany was in her element.

She'd always known this was the life she wanted—interesting conversation, gracious service, elegant surroundings and breathtaking fashions from around the world. Helping her parents with parties had always been fun, but it was nothing compared to the rush of being the hostess herself.

She caught Harrison's smile from across the room, and she could tell she was making him proud. She asked Ambassador Beauregard a question about his family, grateful yet again that her parents had sent her to school in France for two years. One of the Saudi princes came toward them, and Brittany drew him into conversation, introducing him to the ambassador and mentioning their mutual interest in impressionist painters.

Then she politely excused herself, having spotted the wife of a German diplomat standing alone near the terrace door.

"Very polished," came a deep voice beside her.

She glanced behind her and came face-to-face with Alex Lindley. "Thank you."

"I'm not sure it was a compliment."

She wasn't going to let him mess with what was a near-perfect evening. "I'm going to take it as one anyway." She kept walking.

"Want me to crack the facade?"

No chance of that. "You disappeared for a while."

He smiled, voice laced with self-satisfaction. "You noticed?"

"No. I noticed that Harrison disappeared. You were more of a…" She timed a significant pause. "A by-product."

"*That* is a crack in that facade," he said.

"Not at all. You don't count since you're not a guest. Something I can help you with?"

"You know that Harrison thinks you're perfect?"

Brittany didn't answer. There was really no need. She and Harrison enjoyed a great deal of mutual respect. It was why their relationship was going to work.

"So are you in love with him?"

She stopped, and drew an exasperated sigh. "You weren't brought up around nice people, were you?"

"I spent many of my formative years with the U.S. navy."

"That explains a lot."

"Where you probably went to the finest schools money could buy."

"Some of them," she acknowledged.

"So what's your excuse?"

"I need no excuse. I'm not being rude."

"Oh, yes, you are."

No. She wasn't. She was simply responding in kind to his provocation.

"Mr. Lindley," she told him. "You can expect to *get* out of a social interaction that which you put *in.*"

"You're turning me on."

Brittany's jaw dropped open. She was honestly speechless. Did Harrison have any idea what kind of a boor he had employed?

"I'm just saying," Alex continued smoothly, leaning slightly forward, his eyes dancing with obvious delight, "if I'm getting out of this conversation what I'm putting in…"

Then, Harrison caught her eye.

He was heading toward them, looking none too happy.

"I believe your comeuppance is on its way," she informed Alex.

"We've got a problem," Harrison said to Alex.

They certainly did.

"What do you need?" asked Alex, his demeanor instantly changing.

"Julia's at the front gate."

That caught Brittany's attention.

She wasn't sure how she felt about Julia. There was something about the passion, no, the *anger* she inspired in Harrison that left Brittany feeling unsettled.

"I thought she left the country this morning," said Alex.

"Apparently, she did not."

"You want me to go down?"

Harrison looked around. His hand went to the back of his neck. "Never mind. I'll go."

Then he smiled courteously at Brittany, reaching down to give her hand a reassuring squeeze. "I'm sorry I've been neglecting you. I'll be right back."

"I've been fine," said Brittany, determined not to be demanding, even though she would have appreciated a little more of Harrison's attention.

"Thank you," he said, with what seemed to be genuine gratitude.

She took comfort in his appreciation, then she and Alex watched him walk away.

They both stared in silence at the empty doorway as minutes ticked by. Brittany knew she should stay back and see to the guests, but curiosity was burning within her.

"I think we should go with him," she finally ventured, hating the shimmer of what could possibly be jealousy, telling herself it would only take a minute.

"I agree," said Alex, putting a hand on the small of her back and guiding her through the crowded hall. "He may need some help."

The man named Nuri glared suspiciously at Julia while she waited in the small gatehouse. His mouth was set in a grim line, his dark eyes piercing beneath his blue turban. She tried not to squirm on the hard wooden chair, and kept her hands tightly folded in her lap.

She felt a whole lot less than welcome here, that was for sure. And she knew she was risking Harrison's temper by showing up on his doorstep. But she didn't have anywhere else to go.

Even if that roadblock hadn't been intended for her—which it likely wasn't, given that she hadn't murdered anyone or stolen a hundred million in gold bullion—her name was probably in the central police computer. All it would have taken was for an officer to type in the particulars of her passport, and, wham, she'd be right back in jail.

At least this way, there was a chance Harrison would help her. Even if Nuri looked as if he might do her in before she had a chance to talk to him.

The door swung open, and she reflexively straightened her spine.

"Where is she?" came Harrison's gravelly voice.

Nuri pointed with his riding crop, and Harrison turned.

She struggled to gauge his mood. But everything about him was neutral. His tone, his expression, his posture. "I thought you were leaving."

"I tried," she answered honestly.

His eyes squinted down with skepticism. "How hard did you try?"

She knew she needed to come clean. If she'd learned anything about Harrison, it was that he liked the truth, the whole truth, and nothing but the truth.

"Robbie and Melanie left this morning," she began. "And then I tried to leave this afternoon." All true. "But there was this roadblock. At the airport."

He planted his butt against the edge of Nuri's desk and crossed his arms over his chest. "And what are you leaving out?"

"Nothing." That was truly how it had happened. There was no reason for him to know she'd voluntarily changed her ticket.

"They wouldn't let you into the airport? Funny, my guests all arrived on time."

Oh, right. She'd left out something important. But she was nervous. Nuri, especially, was making her nervous.

"The doorman at the hotel," she quickly elaborated. "He said the police were looking for me. *That's* why I was afraid of the roadblock at the airport."

"Are you making this up as you go along?"

"No!"

Harrison straightened away from the desk and moved toward her, definite skepticism in his tone this time. "And why would the police be looking for you?"

She stood to lessen their height difference. She didn't much like it when he loomed over her. Plus, this part was definitely not her fault.

"I don't know *why* they were looking for me. I thought you—" She cut herself off, remembering Nuri. Then she dropped her voice to a hissing whisper. "I thought you took care of that little thing."

"I did," said Harrison. "What else did you do?"

"Nothing. *Nothing.*"

"I have a hard time believing that."

"Yeah? Well, you seem to have a hard time believing anything I say."

They stared at each other for a long minute.

Then, apparently, he got tired of having an audience, because he latched on to her arm. "Out here."

She scrambled out the door with him, along a stone pathway that led over his lawn to a garden gazebo dotted with tables and lawn chairs.

Hands on her upper arms, he sat her down on a padded chair.

"Start from the beginning," he demanded.

There was that height difference again.

"Sit," she told him, gesturing to the next chair.

His lips compressed into a line.

"This feels like the Spanish Inquisition."

"No, it doesn't. And you came to me, remember?"

"Only because I had nowhere else to go."

Then she could have kicked herself for the sarcastic tone. She was asking this man for help. The least she could do was be civil about it.

"I'm sorry," she said. "You're not the Spanish Inquisition."

"I can't help you if you don't tell me what this is all about." But then he did sit down.

Julia took a breath. She went through it from the beginning, all of it—changing her ticket, the doorman, the checkpoint, finally coming to Cadair.

At the end of the hurried explanation, he sat back and gazed across the palm-tree-dotted gardens.

Julia became aware of music coming from the palace. She glanced up and saw lights streaming from every window, flickering lanterns on the veranda and guests, many, many guests both outside and in. It was then that she realized Harrison looked even more formal than usual.

In fact, he was wearing a tux, with a ribboned medal of some kind pinned to his lapel.

"You're having a party." she stated.

He glanced over his shoulder at the palace. "I am."

"I'm sorry."

"That you interrupted my party?"

She nodded.

He coughed out a cold laugh. "I think that's the least of our worries at the moment."

"Is it a special party?"

He raised a brow. "Now who's the Spanish Inquisition?"

"There must be three hundred people in there."

"It's the secretary-general's reception for the United Nations International Economic Summit."

She pasted her gaze on the glittering crowd, suddenly feeling as if she'd fallen into another dimension. "You're kidding."

"No. I am not kidding."

She was so out of her league here. No wonder she and Harrison had a hard time understanding each other.

He cracked a grim half smile. "This part is the reason your arrival caused us so much grief. Had you only been a horse thief, my life would have been a whole lot simpler."

She blinked her focus back to Harrison. "I don't understand." Was he sorry she hadn't been after his horse?

"I thought you were a covert operative sent here to assassinate a Syrian diplomat."

Julia had no response to that.

She honestly could not think of a single thing to say.

Wait a minute. Her heart sank. "You don't think the police—"

"No, no." Harrison vehemently shook his head. "Alex and I were the only ones who even thought of it."

"You can't be sure."

"Yes, I can. Other than the guests and their own security staff, very few people even know about this party. Besides." He paused. "If somebody else thought you were a spy, it wouldn't be the police out looking for you."

Julia swallowed.

She struggled to find her voice. "There was a road-block."

"That likely had nothing to do with you." But then his expression turned contemplative. "You say they came to your hotel?"

It was her turn to nod. "Does that seem like a lot of trouble for a suspected horse thief?"

"I'm afraid so," he agreed.

"You sure they don't think I'm a spy?"

Footsteps clattered on the gazebo steps, and Julia's heart wedged in her throat.

"There you are," came Alex's voice.

He came to a halt with Brittany by his side.

She was dressed in a metallic silver gown, full-length, with a gorgeous, flowing hemline around strappy sandals. The bodice was snug, while the neck was a wide band of exquisitely embroidered netting, decorating her shoulders and chest with gold, looped threads, and gold-and-silver beading.

Her hair was upswept, with a small jeweled comb, while enormous diamonds twinkled on her ears and at her right wrist. She looked as though she'd stepped off a Paris runway.

Julia's pleated, gray skirt and matching bolero jacket felt staid and frumpy. Her canvas flats didn't help the situation, either.

"Is everything okay?" asked Alex.

"Wouldn't Ms. Nash prefer to come inside?" asked Brittany.

Julia looked at Harrison, uncertain what to tell the two.

"Julia's hit a spot of trouble," said Harrison.

Brittany's expression instantly turned concerned. She sat down in the chair directly across from Julia. "Can I help?"

"What kind of trouble?" asked Alex, his hand wrapping around the metal crossbar of Brittany's chair.

And then Julia remembered he was a lawyer. Would he be under any obligation to turn her in?

"For some reason the police are looking for her," said Harrison.

"But you—" Alex cut himself off, his gaze taking a telltale flick toward the top of Brittany's head.

"I'm sure it's a simple mix-up," said Harrison heartily. Julia guessed he was speaking for Brittany's benefit. "But could you make a couple of discreet inquiries?"

"Of course," said Alex.

"I'm sure you'd be more comfortable in the house," said Brittany. "We can go in through the back. You don't have to join the rest of the party."

Her expression told Julia she wasn't stupid. Harrison and Alex might not want to talk in front of her, but she got that they were hiding Julia from what might not be such a simple mix-up.

There was another clatter on the gazebo stairs, these footfalls light and fast.

All heads turned toward the sound.

It was Leila. She was panting, and her eyes were round in the dim light.

"The police," she gasped. "They're at the gate."

Chapter Seven

Harrison jumped to his feet, while Julia froze in place. The dank jail cell rose in her mind again, and she could feel the scratchy cloth against her bare skin.

"I'll go," said Alex.

Brittany rose, as well. "I'll come with you."

Both men opened their mouths to protest.

"I'll join you," said Brittany in a tone of steel. "I am the hostess, and they will be forced to treat *all* of my questions with respect."

Alex looked to Harrison, and Harrison nodded, obviously realizing Brittany intended to slow the police down. "That's a good idea."

Leila spoke again. This time to Julia. "My father says I should take you to the barn."

"Your father?"

"Nuri," said Harrison.

Julia's eyes widened. Were they crazy? Nuri had probably set a trap for her. In fact, he'd probably called the police himself.

"It's safe," said Harrison.

"But—"

"He's loyal to me. It's safe."

Julia wasn't so sure. But as Alex and Brittany set off for the gatehouse, she rose shakily to her feet.

Leila led the way. "My father suggests you go to the vet's office. I'll saddle up Roc and Cedar Twist. If the worst comes…"

"No lights," said Harrison.

Leila shook her head. "I won't need them."

"If the worst comes, what?" asked Julia, glancing from one to the other.

Harrison answered her. "We'll ride into the desert."

She looked over her shoulder at the far-off gatehouse. "You mean they might not go away?"

"I mean, they might search the property."

And she'd be fleeing into the night?

With Harrison or Leila?

Would they get lost in the desert? Die of thirst out there?

And how the hell was she going to get out of the country if they were in the middle of the desert?

Before she could voice any of her questions, Leila opened a side door to the main barn, and they slipped inside.

Harrison took hold of Julia's hand.

She tried not to give away her fear by gripping tight, but she couldn't help herself. If the police found her, they'd take her back to jail.

"Is there a bathroom in here?" she whispered.

Harrison wrapped an arm around her shoulders.

"We'll meet you at the vet's office," he said to Leila.

"Ten minutes," Leila responded, and then her footfalls disappeared down the main hallway.

Julia blinked, but all she could make out was the dark bars of the nearest stalls. The horses shifted and snorted in the depths of the barn while the tang of hay and manure hit her nostrils.

"This way," said Harrison, guiding her to the left.

"Can you see?" she asked.

"Enough. Do you really need the loo?"

"Yes."

"Do you have some kind of problem?"

"No! I have perfectly normal bodily functions. But they don't seem to allow for that in UAE jails."

"You're urinating in case they take you back to jail."

"Yes," she admitted.

Harrison sighed audibly. "Don't be pessimistic."

How could she help but be pessimistic? They'd practically stormed Harrison's gate.

"Who are they?" she asked. "*Why* are they here? I didn't *do* anything."

"Let's let Alex do his job. He'll fix it."

"What if he can't fix it?"

"You're getting ahead of yourself."

"But what if he can't fix it, and they search the place?"

"Then we'll leave."

"Into the desert?"

"Yes."

"Won't they chase us?" Julia couldn't help picturing herself as a player in some kind of desert action flick. The kind where the thirsty, battered, innocent protagonists were trapped in blind canyons by the corrupt cops who had automatic weapons.

Harrison was silent.

"Here's the ladies'," he finally said.

"Thank you." She felt her way into the small room and closed the door. She'd better get ready for another trip to jail, considering their chances of outrunning the police force seemed dismally small.

Perhaps Harrison would be so kind as to teach her the word for *bathroom* in Arabic.

Afterward, she felt her way back out the door.

"Feel better?" he asked.

"Not much."

"Listen." He put a hand on either side of her, trapping her against the wooden wall.

The rough boards dug into her shoulders and her rear end.

He leaned in close so she could just make out his features. "I am not going to let them arrest you."

There was a certainty in his eyes and a determination in his chin that, against all logic, gave her a welcome boost of confidence.

"You might not have a choice," she pointed out.

"I have more choices than most."

"Because you're wealthy."

There was a pause. "Yes."

Of course.

It was a whole other world when you were wealthy.

Unfortunately, Julia wasn't.

She wasn't even all that strong. She didn't want this to be happening to her. She impulsively placed her palm on his chest. The rhythmic beat of his heart pulsed with life, and she willed some of his strength to seep into her body.

He closed his eyes for a split second, and the muscles in his shoulders bunched. His heartbeat deepened, and his scent swirled out around her.

The passion from the pool house invaded her body. Fear and desire coalesced to one emotion, and her focus shifted to his mouth. Just once, she thought. Just once before her life went to hell.

His lips parted and he dipped his head.

Her hand curled into a fist with his shirt trapped inside. She pulled herself up on her toes, slanting her head, tipping forward.

His hand wrapped around the back of her head and dragged her in.

His lips met hers, full on, hot and open.

Passion welled to life from her belly, roiling out to every finger and toe. She opened her mouth, and his tongue invaded. His free arm wrapped around her waist, clutching her firmly to his body, her breasts plastered against him, her belly molding to the shape of his arousal, her thighs flush up against his, not a centimeter between them.

His kiss went to her neck, her ear, her temple, then back to her mouth. He stroked her cheek, ran his hand over her hair, slid the other over her buttocks, kissing her over and over again.

Then something banged in the barn.

A horse, most likely.

But they both jolted back to reality.

He broke the kiss and held her tight, gasping beside her ear, one hand still clasping her bottom.

"Not good," he rasped.

"Sorry," she breathed against his chest.

He shook his head. "That wasn't your fault."

"It was the fear," she said.

"Yeah," he agreed, his grasp on her loosening slowly.

"Could have happened to anyone." She forced herself to pull back.

"The heat of the moment," he said.

"Exactly." She brushed the wrinkles from the front of his dress shirt.

He took a half step back. "There's no need—"

"It never happened."

Harrison could carry on with his plans for an arranged marriage to Brittany without any fear of Julia being indiscreet. It was definitely the least she could do.

Harrison took another step back, and they separated completely.

"The vet's office," he said.

She nodded.

He started to take her hand again, but then backed off.

Good thinking.

Clearly, they couldn't be trusted together.

Harrison had a lot of faith in Alex. And if Alex was suspicious, then so was Harrison.

"Something's not right," Alex repeated, standing next to Brittany in the small vet's office.

Leila had arrived, reporting that the horses were ready to go out the back way if needed. And it was looking as though they might be needed.

"A person of significance?" he parroted Alex's earlier words back to him.

"It usually means some kind of hostile, material

witness," said Alex. "And they only use it in a very serious case."

Harrison's attention went back to Julia. She looked absolutely terrified, but he still didn't know if he could trust her completely. She'd lied to him before.

"Do you have *any* idea what this is about?"

"I've only been here four days," she all but wailed.

"Shh," he admonished. The police were searching in the house at the moment, but they'd move to the barn soon enough.

Her voice turned to a hoarse whisper. "You were with me for most of that time."

"The horse theft charges are back," Alex put in. "It looks to me like they're using anything and everything they can think of to get their hands on Julia."

"Why?" Harrison asked out loud, stymied.

Everyone was silent.

"Somebody thinks she knows something," Alex ventured.

Harrison stared at his friend. Unspoken was that the *somebody* who thought she knew something had the power to influence the UAE law enforcement. Not good for Julia.

"The horses?" asked Leila.

Brittany spoke up. "They'll see you. They'll follow you."

Harrison and Alex looked at each other. Brittany was likely right.

"Unless," Brittany continued. She turned her attention to Julia, sizing the woman up. "Trade me clothes. In case the taxi driver described you."

Julia shook her head. "I can't let you—"

"Oh, yes, you can," said Harrison. He nodded approvingly at Brittany. "A decoy."

"Damn," said Alex with clear admiration.

Brittany's fingers went to the zipper at the side of her gown.

"Men outside, please," came Leila's scolding voice, and Harrison realized he'd been staring.

He and Alex immediately moved into the hallway and shut the door behind them.

"What in the bloody hell is going on?" asked Harrison as soon as they were alone.

Alex shook his head. "Something to do with Millions to Spare?"

"What could she know? What is there to know?"

"It must be connected to Leopold's Legacy."

Harrison switched to that angle. "And somebody knows she was here with the Prestons?"

"And that she followed Millions to Spare."

Harrison swore. There was no telling how high or how far this went. And maybe Julia did know something. But maybe it was something she didn't even realize she knew.

He didn't want to consider the possibility she was playing him again.

No. He wasn't going to explore that line of thinking.

"Want me to sleuth around?" asked Alex.

"Absolutely. When you and Brittany get back—"

"Whoa. Wait a minute. *Me* and Brittany?"

"Julia's my responsibility. And I'm not about to let you get arrested for aiding and abetting a criminal."

Alex looked aghast at the prospect of staying with Brittany.

Good grief. Brittany was a perfectly nice person.

"They're going to follow you two," said Harrison.

"Lead them south as far as you can, then play dumb. I'm going to take the Jeep and go cross-country toward Fujairah."

"Over the dunes?"

"And through the mountains."

Alex cocked his head. "I don't think they'll expect that."

"That's what I'm counting on."

Harrison felt around in his pocket and retrieved a credit card, holding it out to Alex between two fingers. "If you get lucky, and make it to Ajman, book a decoy hotel room with this."

Alex took the card and grinned. "And then book the real one with cash?"

"You got it," said Harrison. "Keep running and keep sleuthing as long as you can. I'll be calling you when I get a chance."

Alex nodded.

The door to the vet's office came open. "They're done," said Leila.

Brittany acknowledged that Julia looked very nice in the Feteami gown. Her breasts were slightly fuller than Brittany's, the result being a more voluptuous silhouette. But there was enough give in the fabric that it still fit her well, and the shimmering beads accentuated Julia's graceful neck.

It would have been better for Brittany's peace of mind if Julia had looked terrible. But Brittany would just have to get over this silly reaction to the woman.

Julia had done nothing overt. She wasn't flirting with Harrison. In fact, Brittany mostly felt sorry for her. She was obviously frightened, and simply wanted to get out of the country as quickly as possible.

Julia teetered a little bit in the four-inch heels. Brittany had to admit she was grateful they'd switched shoes so that she wore the roomy, canvas flats.

She had no desire to go riding through the desert in her Claudio Merazzi shoes. Bad enough she was wearing a dress. She knew her thighs would rub against the saddle, but hopefully they wouldn't be out there too long. And she could climb into the big, en suite bathtub when they got back.

She could already feel the soothing, foamy water.

She was worried there wouldn't be a proper goodbye for the guests at the secretary-general's party. But she supposed that couldn't be helped. Although she didn't have a diamond on her finger as yet, it was her job to support Harrison.

She drew a deep breath as the men walked back into the office. In this, she was ready, willing and able to offer support.

"Thank you," Julia offered, reaching out to squeeze Brittany's hand.

Brittany smiled at the woman and squeezed back. If it wasn't for the odd energy she sensed between Julia and Harrison, she might even like the woman.

"It'll be over soon," she promised.

"Oh, I hope so," said Julia.

There was a faint buzz, and Leila grabbed her cell phone from her pocket and put it to her ear.

"They're coming," she whispered to the group. Then she pointed to an outside exit door from the little office. "I'll explain to your grandmother, and Darla will make sure the guests get a proper goodbye."

"Tell her the French, the Uzbeks—" He swore under his breath.

"Darla will know what to do," said Leila. "She'll tell them the right story."

Harrison gave a grim-faced nod, and Brittany understood there must be some important diplomatic talks going on at the party.

"Roc and Cedar Twist are this way," said Leila.

Knowing time was running out, Brittany headed for the door.

To her surprise, Alex appeared at her elbow.

"What—"

"Shh."

"But—"

"Quiet," he ground out as he ushered her through the exit to the dark yard. "You need help getting on?"

"No." She had been riding since she was five years old. She was perfectly capable of mounting her own horse.

But where the heck was Harrison?

She strained to look over her shoulder.

Leila shut the door, and she and Alex were alone, save for the two horses tied to the hitching post.

"Where's Harrison?" she demanded.

Alex grinned as he untied the lead rope of the taller animal. "He's with Julia."

"What?"

"Quiet," Alex warned.

"You're coming with *me?"* Brittany couldn't believe it. She was sacrificing her thighs to spend time with Alex?

"We'll both be taking a ride with the police if you don't get on that horse." He mounted and turned his big chestnut in a circle.

Some lights went on in the building behind them, and

Brittany deftly released the other lead rope. She swung up on the mare, adjusted her seat, arranged the skirt as best she could and took up the reins.

"How did you pull this off?" she asked Alex in the most accusatory voice she could muster.

He just grinned unrepentantly at her. "Looks like it's you and me, babe." Then he turned south along the fence line and urged the horse to a gallop.

Brittany spurred her horse to follow. She was going to kill Alex. The second she had an opportunity, she was simply going to kill him.

Julia struggled to keep up with Harrison, crossing his lush lawn in the ridiculous high-heeled shoes.

Brittany had smaller feet.

She was marrying Harrison, and she had smaller feet.

Julia gritted her teeth in frustration with herself.

She had to stop caring about the stupid things. She was in a foreign country, and she was running from the police. What did she care about Brittany's shoe size or what Harrison saw in the woman?

Of course, it could be that Brittany was beautiful, cultured, gracious and kind. Oh, yeah. And intelligent. Brittany seemed very intelligent.

She supposed a man might be interested in some of those qualities.

Not to mention that Brittany had a title. She was Lady Brittany Livingston. Julia had looked it up on her laptop back at the hotel. No reason to look her up, really, other than plain old curiosity. Harrison was practically going into an arranged marriage with Lady Livingston, and Julia had wondered why he would do that.

Harrison stopped abruptly at the corner of an out-building, and Julia all but stumbled into the back of him. His hand clamped firmly around her wrist. He was holding a little tighter than was comfortable, but she wasn't about to complain. He'd make sure she didn't fall, and he knew exactly where they were going on this dark, moonless night.

"See that yard light?" He pointed to a spot in the distance.

"Is that where we're going?" She was disappointed by the distance. There was already a blister forming on her baby toe.

"No," said Harrison, and she breathed a sigh of relief.

"We have to avoid it," he continued. "We'll go around the back of that paddock, and come up on the garage from the south."

"You're joking."

He turned to look at her. "What do you mean?"

"I mean, my feet are killing me."

He glanced down. "So take off your shoes."

That solution seemed a little too simple.

"Won't I cut my feet?"

"On grass?"

"What about poisonous snakes?"

"Vipers?"

Julia shuddered.

"I'd worry more about scorpions," said Harrison.

"Oh, thanks."

"I was joking. Vipers like the sand, and scorpions are usually under rocks."

"That really wasn't funny, Harrison."

"Take off your shoes."

"Seriously. We're running for our lives here. At least

my life. Well, my freedom. And you're making jokes about *poisonous* things."

"Venomous things."

"I hate you."

"No, you don't."

Of course she didn't. He was rescuing her. But he didn't have to be such a jerk about it.

"Take off your shoes," he repeated.

But she couldn't bring herself to do it. Even if snakes and scorpions were rare on manicured lawns, she wasn't dashing around in the pitch-dark not knowing *what* she might be stepping on.

He let go of her wrist, turned his back and crouched down. "Then hop on."

"I'm not—"

"Blisters, scorpions or me. Unless you'd rather deal with the police."

Without another word, Julia hiked up her skirt and clambered onto his back.

He grunted and shifted her into place, wrapping his hands around her bare thighs before straightening.

"Hang on tight," he warned, and then he started to jog.

There was nothing but her panties between her and his suit. Nothing at all between his hands and her thighs. She could smell his hair, hear his deep breathing, feel the shift and play of his muscles.

And then, there was the friction.

Oh, the friction.

She tried to shift, to get away from it, to alleviate the embarrassing—

"Hold *still*," he commanded.

She froze.

Unfortunately, he kept moving, and the feeling began to throb between her legs.

What was she, a danger junkie or something? First the kiss and now this? If she wasn't careful, she was going to—

"How can you be getting tired?" he asked.

"I'm not tired."

"You're panting in my ear."

"Sorry." She tried to get her mind on something else. Poor Millions to Spare. Or poor Leopold's Legacy, ready, willing and waiting to race.

Or the jail cell.

Or the police.

She glanced behind her.

Thankfully, she didn't see floodlights or dogs or an army of uniforms hot on their heels.

A shot of adrenaline went through her again, and she buried her face in the crook of Harrison's neck. What if he couldn't get them out of this? What happened then?

She tightened her hold on him, inhaling his scent, convincing herself he was some kind of superman who could face down any danger, solve any problem. And then the pulse started again, and the friction, and the longing.

He came to a halt and slid her down off his back.

She all but groaned at the sensation.

"Stay nice and quiet," he whispered.

She nodded, not trusting herself to open her mouth. Every nerve ending was on fire for him.

He took her hand. "There are four cars in the garage. The one at the far end is the Jeep. I won't be turning on the lights. But the door's going to make quite a lot of noise when we open it. Not to mention the motor of the Jeep."

Not to mention Julia if she didn't get her body calmed down.

"I hope they followed Alex and Brittany. And the music should cover our sound. But if they start to chase us, *hang on tight.* And for God's sake, do up your seat belt."

Julia nodded again.

He looked at her closely. "Are you all right?"

"Fine," she managed, her pulse finally slowing, her body coming back under control.

"Good to hear." He slowly opened the door.

They passed through, and he pointed her in the direction of the Jeep. "Feel your way along the wall. I'm going to fill a water bottle and pull a few other things together."

She tripped a couple of times over unseen objects in the dark, but managed to feel her way past one, two, then three cars. She found the Jeep, and made her way into the passenger side, fastening her seat belt tight.

She heard Harrison at the driver's side. He shoved some gear into the backseat.

"Are you ready?" he asked.

She nodded, then realized he couldn't see her. "Yes."

She heard a click, then a groan and a whine, and the overhead door in front of them cranked upward.

The lights from the palace appeared, then the palm trees, then the stars. So far, nobody seemed to have raised an alarm.

Harrison started the engine and eased their way out. His profile came clear as he hit the garage-door remote, and the door whined shut again behind them.

Still driving slowly, he turned them away from the palace.

So far, so good.

They crossed the lawn, then followed a rutted track down a sloping hill, and the buildings disappeared behind them.

She watched over her shoulder, then looked at Harrison. "Did we do it?"

"Maybe. I'm not sure yet."

Then a pair of headlights appeared on the hill, rocking airborne at the crest, then slamming down onto the rutted tracks.

"Hang on," Harrison called, yanking the gearshift and revving the engine.

Chapter Eight

Harrison pointed the Jeep toward the northeast corner of his property. He knew how to find a short, dirt road that would take them to a small wadi. They'd cross it, and then they'd be onto the dunes.

He glanced at the bouncing lights in the rearview mirror. Whoever was behind him was in a sedan. So they wouldn't be following onto the desert. Well, hopefully, they'd follow about twenty meters or so, then sink to the axles.

Putting the Jeep into third, he spared a quick glance at Julia. She was white as a ghost, her eyes wide in the dim light, and her hands squeezed the armrests in a death grip.

"Will they shoot at us?" she rasped.

"I certainly hope not."

Oops. Bad answer. She looked even more terrified, if that was possible, shrinking down in her seat.

"Nobody is going to shoot at us," he assured her, even though he wasn't sure it was true. He couldn't worry about bullets at the moment. He turned his attention back to the terrain.

"You should turn me in," Julia shouted to him above the noise of the bouncing vehicle.

"I don't think so," he responded as they picked up the dirt road.

"You're going to be in trouble."

"Not if we get away."

"Won't they radio ahead?" She'd seen enough car-chase movies to know about roadblocks, spike strips and air surveillance.

"They won't be putting up a roadblock on the sand dunes," he said.

The ground fell away, and he made a sharp right turn on the goat track that would take him to the bottom of Wadi Wasmi.

Julia gasped as the Jeep fishtailed, the tires spitting out sand and rocks, before getting traction on the bumpy trail.

Harrison gave the sedan a fifty-fifty chance of making the turn. He grabbed second gear, bouncing wildly in his seat. Julia was staring straight ahead at the headlight beams flashing on rocks, sand and the occasional boulder or outcrop.

He wrestled the steering wheel, keeping them on course, until they finally made it to the relatively smooth surface at the bottom. Then, he dared to glance in the rearview mirror, pressing on the accelerator, and bringing the Jeep up a gear.

The sedan had made the turn, but it was forced to slow down on the trail. Good. He was bringing them out on the dunes behind Hebba Hill. He hoped they'd have radio trouble after they got stuck.

Julia turned to watch him.

"You're crazy," she said.

He couldn't help but grin. "Are you wishing you'd taken your chances with the police?" He watched carefully for the signs of the track that would take them up the other side of the wadi.

She glanced at the headlights behind. "Not exactly. But this isn't looking so good."

"I have a plan," said Harrison, as he spotted the trail.

He jerked left on the wheel, bouncing them up a trail equally rough and steep. Julia shut up and hung on, while he glanced at the tachometer to optimize each gear.

They were down into first before they crested the hill. It was a short fifty meters before the rocks and packed dirt gave way to full-on sand. Harrison used the time to get his speed up, hitting the dunes, fishtailing for a moment before he settled in, then streaking off across the unbroken desert.

"Watch out behind us," he told Julia. "Tell me what happens."

She swiveled in her seat, stretching her arm across the back.

"Nothing," she said. Then, "Wait. I see headlights. They're out of the valley. Speeding up. Coming." She paused.

"Did they make it to the sand?"

"I think they might be stuck."

Harrison smacked the steering wheel with his palm. "Yes!"

She turned to him. "That was your plan?"

"That was my plan."

"What about planes?"

He shook his head. "Planes are unlikely. Even if they wanted to send one up, it would take quite a while to get it here, and this is a very big desert. They have no idea which way we'll go."

All in all, he was feeling pretty satisfied.

Then her small hand covered his on the gearshift.

He warned himself not to react to her touch, nor to react to the contrast of her pale, delicate hand against his rough, larger one.

"I can't let you do this," she said in a voice that was both brave and terrified at the same time.

"It's done."

"No, it's not done. They know who you are. They know where you live. You're a fugitive from justice."

"I'm taking a pretty girl out for a ride in the desert. I don't believe there's a law against that."

"Nobody's going to believe you didn't notice the police car in high-speed pursuit."

"Who's to say that was a police car?"

She compressed her lips, eyes narrowing in annoyance.

"Seriously, Julia. We do not know that was a police car."

"It was. And eventually you'll have to go home. And I can't let you put yourself in trouble for me."

"As I told you before, I have options."

She drew in a shuddering breath. "Turn around, Harrison. Let's go back."

He chuckled. "Right. Because I'm not already in trouble."

"You can tell them—"

"Julia."

"You can explain that—"

"Shut up." He reached into the pocket of his jacket, extracting the red booklet he kept on him at all times.

He tossed it into her lap. "Get out of jail free card," he told her.

Her hand left his, and she picked the booklet up. "What?"

"Diplomatic passport."

"Who *are* you?"

He took a breath.

"Yeah, yeah, yeah," she said, with a dismissive wave of her hand. "The Right Honorable Lord Harrison William Arthur Beaumont-Rochester, Baron Welsmeire."

"I get a kick out of the fact you can remember all that."

"Why do you have a diplomatic passport?"

"I'm a special ambassador to the UAE."

"And they can't put you in jail."

"They can't put me in jail. They can send me home. But that's a pretty big gun. They would run the risk of causing an international incident by sending me back to Britain." This time, he reached out and covered her hand. "I can't see them doing that over charges of attempted horse theft. Particularly when I was the victim."

But then Harrison frowned to himself. Truth was, he couldn't see them chasing Julia and him through the desert over those charges, either. Something strange was happening here, and it was something that had little to do with the enforcement of law in UAE.

Somebody was after Julia. And, Alex was right, Millions to Spare and Leopold's Legacy had to be involved. Either Julia knew something, or somebody thought she knew something. Either way, Harrison had to keep her out of their hands until he could figure out what was going on.

Brittany was grateful when Alex finally decided the horses were getting tired. She'd been exhausted for an hour, and her inner thighs were burning from the friction of the leather saddle. She gritted her teeth, dismounting slowly and painfully.

The horse grew impatient, and shifted, and she grabbed for the saddle horn.

"Whoa." Alex was beside her in an instant, bracing her from behind.

She gasped as one of his hands contacted her chafed skin. But his support allowed her to get safely to the ground.

"You okay?" he asked, stepping back to stare worriedly down at her.

"Fine," she told him, brushing off the skirt and settling the soft shoes back on her feet. She was sweaty and sticky, and her thighs were going to take days to heal. Not to mention the fact that she smelled like a horse.

This was not what she'd pictured when she'd agreed to visit Harrison. She sucked in a thick breath of the sultry midnight air. It wasn't what she'd pictured at all.

"We can stow the saddles." Alex nodded toward an abandoned hut on the opposite side of the dusty road. "And put the horses in the paddock. I'll call Nuri later and let him know where to find them."

Then he gazed up and down the dark road. "What do you think? We've come fifteen, twenty miles?"

"I have no idea," said Brittany, debating whether to unsaddle Cedar Twist or leave that chore for Alex.

"I think we're a little way west of Route Eleven. But I'm not sure how far…"

"Are we lost?" In the end, she took pity on the horse, edging carefully over to it and reaching for the cinch.

"We're not lost. I'd just like to give the taxi a precise location." He flipped open his cell phone.

Brittany's heart sighed at the thought of a taxi. A lovely, soft-seated, air-conditioned taxi that would take them back to Cadair and her lovely, large bathtub. She'd have something tall and cool, an iced tea, or maybe champagne and orange juice. They'd served some flakey almond croissants earlier, and she was starving. The party was probably over by now, but surely they could rustle up something.

Visions of frosted glasses and ice cubes dancing in her head, she heard Alex speaking Arabic on the phone. Then he clicked it off and stuck it back in his tuxedo pocket.

"Why didn't you call someone at Cadair?" she asked.

"They might be monitoring the phones."

"Oh." She pulled off the saddle.

Alex quickly lifted it from her arms.

"Then, won't they check the taxi?"

Halfway to the little hut, he looked back over his shoulder. "What do you mean?"

"I mean, when it drops us off at Cadair, the police are going to see us."

"The taxi's taking us to a hotel." He continued his journey, climbing the single step and pushing open the pale-green door that hung on one hinge.

A hotel?

Well. She supposed that made sense. And she could live with a hotel. Just, please, let them have a nice suite available, with a whirlpool tub and twenty-four-hour room service.

"Are we going into Dubai?"

"To Ajman." Alex went to work on the other horse. "It's closer, and I want to leave a trail of bread crumbs."

Brittany watched him work efficiently on the buckles and straps of Roc's saddle. Even the expensive tuxedo couldn't make him look civilized. His shoulders were too broad, his chest too deep. He had big, rough hands, a darkly defined brow, a broad nose and the kind of square chin that would make other men think twice about crossing him.

"So you're an American," she ventured.

He cracked a small smile. "I'm an American."

"How did you meet Harrison?"

"He advertised for an international lawyer." Alex straightened and effortlessly lifted the saddle from the big animal. "We have newspapers in America, you know. And I do read."

She ignored his sarcasm. "I thought you said you were a soldier."

"I was a soldier." He crossed the road to the shack once more, talking over his shoulder while he walked. "When I wasn't busy shooting people, I studied law."

"They let you do that?" she called.

"Yes, ma'am, they let us study pretty much whatever we want." He walked through the door, then shortly returned. "As long as we keep shooting people in our off-hours, of course."

She nodded. "Of course."

He went to work on Cedar Twist's bridle. "You do know I'm joking, right?"

No, she hadn't. "You're not a lawyer?"

"No, I don't shoot people. You don't go to law school during the day and shoot people in the evenings."

"Oh." Well, she hadn't assumed he meant every evening. "Then, what *did* you do?"

He crossed to Roc, removing the stallion's bridle, as well. "I was involved in the Gulf War, early on, aerial reconnaissance."

"You fly planes?"

"Yes. I prefer that to killing people."

She fought a smile. "Good to know."

He gathered up the two bridles and gave her a nod. "I would think so. What with the two of us all alone out here on this deserted little road." Then he turned once more toward the shack.

She stared after him in frozen silence, suddenly hyperaware of the quiet, the heat, his excruciatingly powerful maleness.

It hadn't occurred to her to question her safety. It certainly hadn't occurred to her to question his intentions.

He exited the shack, looming closer, his feet sending up small puffs of dust into the still air, his powerful arms swinging with his determined walk, his dark eyes watching her.

"Oh, hell," he spat out, making her jump. "I was *joking.* I didn't mean to scare you."

She tossed her head. "I'm not scared."

He stopped in front of her, hands going to his hips. "I protect people," he stated, the offense clear in his tone. "I would never, *ever,* not in a million years, harm a defenseless woman."

It occurred to Brittany that his words would ring a lot truer if he wasn't shouting them at her.

* * *

Julia moaned loudly, folding her arms on the dashboard of the Jeep and dropping her sweaty forehead onto them. "I'm *melting*."

The sun had cleared the eastern mountains two hours ago, but Harrison refused to run the air-conditioning. He claimed it wasted fuel. And while she was firmly *against* the idea of running out of gas in the middle of a desert, she was also firmly against the idea of dying of heatstroke with the Jeep still running.

"Buck up," said Harrison. "I don't think it's more than ninety-five." The sleeves of his dress shirt were rolled up, and he'd long since discarded his tux jacket and bow tie.

"But we're in an oven." She sat up and gestured to the heat waves rolling up off the sand. "We're actually cooking!" She tugged at the collar of her dress. "And I'm wrapped in foil."

Harrison started to laugh.

"Don't," she barked at him. Whatever the metallic fabric was, it held in every ounce of heat and moisture. "I swear, I'm going to rip this thing off my body."

"Be my guest," he said. Then he nodded ahead down the faint sand track. "But you might want to have something on when we meet up with them."

Her gaze darted out the windshield.

Half a dozen colorfully dressed men on horseback were riding toward them. The troop looked like something straight out of *Arabian Nights*.

"Bandits?" she asked Harrison, her sweat suddenly turning cold.

"I have no idea," said Harrison. "There are a lot of different tribes out here, doing a lot of different things in the desert."

"Are they dangerous?" Their windows were all down, and the fabric top of the Jeep offered little protection if somebody meant them harm.

"Looks like we're about to find out."

The group drew closer, kicking up dust and revealing a camel amongst the horses. If Julia wasn't so frightened, she might have appreciated the fascinating spectacle.

As it was, she held her breath while the riders separated around the Jeep, passing by on either side. Harrison didn't slow down, which Julia thought was exceedingly wise.

When the last of them streamed past, she allowed herself a sigh of relief. Perhaps they were merely fellow travelers, moving from one village to the next.

"Uh-oh," Harrison muttered, glancing in the rearview mirror and pushing his foot down on the accelerator.

"What?" Julia twisted her head.

They were coming back.

"This can't be good," she intoned.

"Tell me about it." He shifted gears.

But the riders were gaining on them, whooping and shrieking in a chantlike fashion. She was pretty sure it wasn't a greeting.

They passed by, arms raised, some with swords, peering in the window, before peeling off to circle around again.

"Be nice if you had a head scarf," said Harrison.

But she had nothing she could use. For the first time today, she was glad of the full coverage provided by the evening gown.

"What do we do?"

"Just what we're doing."

And then she saw him.

Outside her window.

His chin was covered, his forehead obscured by a white-and-blue headdress. But she recognized his nose, and those piercing eyes, and the uneven eyebrows.

And then he peeled away, like the others, circling back around for another pass.

"Holy shit," said Julia, whooshing back in her seat.

"What?"

"I know that man."

"How?" Harrison demanded. "Why?"

"From the track. He gave me Millions to Spare's name. He thought I was placing a bet."

Harrison stared at her for a moment.

"Hang on," he said, gearing down, popping the clutch and increasing his speed.

The Jeep rattled frighteningly, but the horses and camels began falling behind. At first they were lost in the dust. And then, as the Jeep reached fifty, she knew they had to be gone.

"It has to be a coincidence," she said, more to herself than to Harrison.

"I don't think so," he said.

She was trying not to panic. She was seriously trying not to panic. "So he went to the track. Lots of people go to the track. Don't they?"

"He learns you're interested in Millions to Spare. Millions to Spare dies, and then he practically ambushes us in the desert? That's one hell of a coincidence."

"It could happen," she insisted.

"You want to bet your life on it?"

Julia stared back at the dust plume funneling out behind them, then turned to the endless desert in front of them.

"Whatever you do," she told Harrison, "don't turn on the air-conditioning."

Chapter Nine

Four hours later, death was beginning to feel preferable to spending another minute in the bouncing Jeep under the broiling desert sun.

Julia was half-asleep—or maybe she was half-delirious from thirst and heatstroke—by the time Harrison stopped the Jeep and killed the engine. She groggily blinked open her eyes. They'd long since run out of water. Dust had scratched her eyeballs raw. It had seeped into her hair, her clothing, her very pores.

Harrison lifted his sunglasses and parked them on top of his short, dark hair. "Are you all right?" he asked in a voice that sounded as raspy as hers felt.

"Great," she answered, bracing her hands on either edge of her bucket seat and easing her body upright. "Where are we?"

"Khandi Oasis. I doubled back." He pocketed the

keys to the Jeep in the breast pocket of his dust-streaked dress shirt. "It should take them a while to find us."

"How long's a while?"

"Hopefully, forever."

She tried to smile at his joke, but her dry lips felt as if they might crack.

She glanced around at the collection of white huts and square buildings set amongst coarse grasses, thorn trees and palms. "Is there a hotel here?"

"Not exactly," said Harrison, setting the brake and reaching for his door handle.

"A tent?" she asked, getting less particular by the second. If it was out of the sun, out of the wind and had any kind of a beverage available, she was in.

"I have a friend here. He may have a cottage we can use."

Julia breathed a sigh of relief. "Lead me to him."

While she pawed at her door handle, Harrison rounded the front of the Jeep to help. He held out a hand while she straightened her reluctant legs. They were decidedly weak as she rolled to her feet.

Then the world began to buzz and spin.

"Uh-oh," Harrison's voice was hollow and distant, and she felt his arms close around her.

She woke up on her back, in a cool room, with a fan turning lazily above her. As she blinked her way back to reality, bright fabrics came into focus against stark, white walls. Woven baskets and hammered silver dotted the tables in the room, while bentwood, rattan chairs were interspersed with vividly colored rugs.

"Welcome back," came Harrison's soft voice, and she turned her head toward the sound.

He smiled down at her. His dark eyes were uncharacteristically warm and kind. She guessed swooning was what a girl had to do to bring out his softer side. Had she known, she could have swooned days ago.

His fingertips touched the cool cloth on her forehead.

"Thirsty?" he asked.

"I guess I passed out."

"That you did."

He slipped an arm beneath her shoulders, propping her up while handing her a glass of water.

She took a few sips of the tepid liquid. "Is there air-conditioning in here?"

"They use it sparingly." He took the glass from her hand and let her lie down again. "The settlement has a generator."

"It feels like heaven."

He sat back in his chair. "I'm glad you approve. We may be here for a while."

Reality crept back into her consciousness. "Are we safe?"

"As safe as I can make us."

She nodded, feeling suddenly emotional and maudlin. "Thank you," she croaked.

"No problem."

She wheezed out a weak laugh. "Right. I can't imagine I've been any trouble at all."

He paused. "You are exciting. I'll give you that."

She willed her strength back, reminding herself they were still in precarious circumstances.

"Exciting is one way to put it." She pushed herself into a sitting position.

He reflexively reached for her, but then backed off when it was clear she wasn't going to keel over.

She took another drink of water.

Gazing down, she realized she was wearing some kind of loose cotton tunic and skirt instead of the evening gown. She blinked at the maroon-and-yellow fabric, layered over the full-length brown skirt. Had Harrison undressed her?

"Yes," he answered her unspoken question.

She wasn't sure how strongly she objected to him undressing her, or even if she objected at all. But she wasn't going to let him know that.

"Well, I sure hope you didn't look," she said.

"I thought about closing my eyes," he responded mildly. "But then I realized I'd have to feel my way around."

"So you ogled me while I was unconscious?" She drank some more water, feeling stronger by the second.

He gave her an enigmatic smile, neither confirming nor denying the accusation.

"Is that what they teach you at Oxford?"

"You were wearing underwear. And you were dying of heat prostration."

Julia reflexively scrambled to remember if her bra and panties matched. Stupid thing to worry about under the circumstances, but she couldn't help herself.

And she really couldn't remember. It had been too long since she'd dressed yesterday, and it was dark when she switched clothes with Brittany.

So she was either wearing a stylish little white set with royal-blue piping, or she'd gone with the comfortable, canary cotton panties with the beige sport bra. She wriggled a little to see if she could tell the difference.

Using a clay pitcher on the table, Harrison refilled her water glass. "You'd rather I'd let you die?"

"I'd rather you'd found a nice, matronly woman to take off my clothes."

She took another drink, unable to stop herself from wondering if, aside from the underwear, Harrison had liked what he saw. Between her busy job and her gym membership in Lexington, she was in pretty good shape. At least she had that going for her. And she had a decent tan. Was he the kind of guy who cared about tan lines?

"We're hiding, remember?" he pointed out. "The fewer people who see us, the better."

He made a good point. She forced herself to set aside thoughts of Harrison and her near-naked body, taking in the room around her, reminding herself she was only temporarily safe. "What is this place?"

"It's a guest cottage. It belongs to Ahmed Hassanat. He's Nuri's brother."

Julia's stomach contracted at the mere mention of the dour man. Maybe she wasn't so safe after all. "I think he's the one who called the police."

"Nuri?"

She nodded.

"That's ridiculous."

"He hates me."

"He doesn't even know you."

"He glares at me so hard, I think he's willing me back to jail."

Harrison grinned.

"It's not funny."

"I doubt Nuri thinks about you one way or the other."

"You didn't see the expression on his face."

"He's a product of a Middle Eastern upbringing forty years ago. He's incredibly chauvinistic."

"So he hates me because I'm a woman?"

"He doesn't hate you. He thinks you're, well, you know."

"Inferior?"

"Not too bright and rather childlike."

Julia could feel her blood pressure going up. She took another swig of water, knowing she'd need her strength.

"Him, not me," Harrison hastily added. "I think that's why his relationship is so strained with Leila."

"I thought Leila grew up in England."

"She went to school there—Nuri's second wife was British," Harrison explained. "When she fell ill, she made Nuri promise to send Leila to school in the West. She died, and Nuri honored her wishes. But he hasn't a clue what to do with Leila now."

There went Julia's blood pressure again. "She's not his property."

"He doesn't dare marry her off to an Arab man," said Harrison. "It would be a disaster."

"What does Leila want?"

Harrison paused. "I doubt he's asked her."

"Have you ever asked her?"

"Oh, of course. Because there's no way that could go bad."

"The girl deserves a chance to live her life." Julia liked Leila.

"Yes, she does. But this is the UAE. Nuri's her father. And we're currently guests in his brother's house."

Julia started to argue further, but then she clamped her jaw. Unfortunately, she was going to have to pick her battles today.

"Clever girl," Harrison said approvingly.

"What do we do now?"

She remembered Harrison saying they'd doubled

back. Did he mean they were on their way back to Cadair? Would it be safe for her in Dubai that quickly?

"We'll spend the night here," said Harrison. "Maybe a couple more days."

"And after that?" She didn't mean to sound demanding, but she needed to get back to the U.S. The sooner, the better.

"I haven't figured that part out yet."

She opened her mouth to pose another question, but then she took in his wrinkled shirt, his sweaty brow and his red-rimmed eyes. An unexpected emotion tightened her chest.

"You should be back with Brittany," she told him. She was sorry he'd been dragged into this. Although, she had to admit, she wasn't sorry he'd ignored her request to take her back last night.

He blew out a breath. "I can't disagree with you on that point."

She steeled herself once more to try to do the right thing. "Is there somewhere…that you could…"

Was she brave enough to offer? Was she principled enough to suggest he walk away and leave her?

Part of her wanted to be principled, but another part of her was scared to death.

"I'm not leaving you," he said.

Thank God. "You should."

He cracked a very small smile. "Do you actually think I could live with myself if I left you to corrupt policemen and unruly mobs?"

"Don't forget about the snakes."

"And, of course, the snakes."

She resisted the urge to reach for him. He had no reason to help her, and yet here he was.

Her throat thickened. "You're a very nice man, you know."

"Don't sound so surprised."

She fought to toss off her emotions. "Well, your staff did have me thrown in jail. And you did try to kill me."

"There is that," he agreed, but laughter lit a glow behind his eyes.

"You wouldn't really have strangled me, would you?"

He shook his head. "Not a chance. I was as angry with myself as I was at you. I thought I'd let you dupe me. I thought I'd fallen for your soft voice and your smooth skin, and let my—"

He cleared his throat.

She thought again about how he'd driven like a maniac through the hot desert sun, carried her from the Jeep, changed her clothes and brought her water. An overwhelming feeling of gratitude invaded her and along with it, emotions she was powerless to stop.

He was a very good man, and she had no business feeling the way she felt about him.

"We're both fools," she said in a quiet voice.

This time, the glow behind his eyes wasn't laughter.

"Yeah." He nodded. "There is that."

Harrison was definitely a fool.

He was sitting here staring at a woman with bare feet, disheveled hair, the plainest of cotton clothing and a half-sunburned face. And all he could think was that she was so beautiful, he wanted to drag her into his arms, kiss those tender lips and make soft, sweet love to her until she forgot everything else in the world.

Leave her?

Not a chance.

He was going to get her to safety or die trying.

He liked to think it was chivalry, but he was beginning to worry it could be something else.

Okay, he was positive that it was at least one other thing—desire. And right now, she was staring at him with those round, crystal-blue eyes. And he knew that she knew. Hell, she'd have to be both blind and amnesiac not to know he wanted her.

Their kiss had been incredible.

Even now, he remembered her smooth skin, her delectable lips, the fresh scent of her hair. His memories moved him subconsciously forward. He breathed her in, while his fingertips feathered her knees, and the warmth of her skin filtered through the rough, cotton dress.

He was going to kiss her again.

He was going to do it now, simply because he had to.

She'd obviously guessed his intentions, because her body tilted toward him in response.

"You're engaged," she breathed, a pained expression flitting across her face.

"Not yet." He hadn't even bought a ring, never mind popped the question.

Her head tilted, and her lips softened. "But you will be."

His hand crept around to the back of her head. "Let's survive this little adventure before—"

"Are we in that much danger?"

He hesitated.

He didn't want to lie. But he knew those men in the desert weren't the police, and they'd looked extremely dangerous.

At his silence, her expression shifted. She wriggled

forward. Her hands rose to cup his cheeks. "If we're in that much danger…"

He sucked in a sharp breath as her lips touched his.

Reaction ricocheted through him. He tangled his fingers in her hair, gripping convulsively at its softness. His free arm snaked around to press against the small of her back. He came to his feet, pulling her with him, bringing their bodies flush together while he deepened the kiss and reveled in passion that consumed his body.

A tidal wave of emotion washed through him. He closed his eyes and let every millimeter of her body imprint itself on his brain. He lowered his hand to her buttocks, pressing her meaningfully into him, letting her know he was aroused—as if there was any question.

His mouth opened wider. His tongue probed deeper. His breathing grew labored. And his hands squeezed her intimately.

He moved his lips to the crook of her neck, and she groaned as he tested the tender skin. Her hands wound around his neck, clinging tight, pressing her breasts against his body, her hardened nipples spurring his desire.

He slipped a hand between them and covered one breast with his palm, reveling in the soft weight and the delicate texture. Her mouth found his again, kissing hard and deep, leaving no question of her acceptance.

Then she fumbled with the buttons on his shirt.

He shrugged out of it, and she pressed her hot lips against his chest. He held still for a moment, palms swirling in her hair, eyes closed, teeth gritted.

Then he pulled off the tunic, flipped the clasp of her bra and gazed at her creamy breasts, topped with perfect, pink nipples. For a second, he couldn't move. He couldn't breathe.

He reached for her breast, watching in fascination as his broad, tanned hand covered the pale mound. Her eyes fluttered closed, and her head tipped back.

He kissed her exposed neck, drawing the skin into the hot cavern of his mouth. She gripped his upper arms to brace herself, fingertips digging into him in a way that ratcheted up his desire. He kissed his way down to one nipple, then the next, drawing the taut pebble into his mouth, laving it with his tongue, trying desperately to hang on to some semblance of control, even as he fought the urge to rip off the rest of her clothes.

Her breaths came in pants.

He pulled at the waistband of her skirt, dragging it over her hips, past her buttocks, down her thighs, until it pooled on the floor.

Then he drew back to gaze at her.

She was drop-dead gorgeous. He'd never seen a more beautiful, more desirable woman. He put his palm flat against her chest. She watched as he eased his way down, over her breast, her flat belly, her hip bone, her downy curls.

She tipped her head up, and met his eyes.

They stared at each other, frozen in time.

Then his free hand went to the button on his slacks.

She didn't blink as he flipped it open. He drew down the zipper. Their last chance to stop, and they both knew it.

Neither of them took it.

He kicked out of his pants, and drew her down on the bed, stretching full length beside her, legs entangling, hands caressing.

He slowed his kisses, touching her face, smoothing her hair, whispering in her ear, using French to tell her she was beautiful and desirable, and he'd never been with a woman who moved him more.

His hands wandered, while hers did the same, discovering secrets and hollows, speeding up their breathing, then slowing it down again.

In French, he told her everything he was doing, everything he was feeling, everything he wanted.

She kissed him deeply, her hands on a journey that forced him to grit his teeth, sweat popping out on his brow.

He needed her. Now. Right now.

His fingertips skimmed their way up her long, smooth legs, and her thighs twitched apart, inviting him. He swiftly extracted a condom from his wallet, positioning his body, feeling the hot, enticing entrance to hers.

He kissed her one more time, entwined their fingers, murmured words of passion and want and desire.

"J'aussi," she whispered breathlessly, flexing her hips.

Before his brain registered her French response, he was inside her, and his world contracted to a single primal urge. He thrust and withdrew, over and over.

A freight train roared and throbbed to life inside his brain, growing faster and louder and harder, in sync with his body. But he held the urgency at bay.

He kissed her deeper. He clasped her to him, feeling the twitches of her body, hearing the gasps of her breath, tasting the pure nectar of her swollen mouth.

She whispered his name.

Then she said it again.

He wanted her to stop, but he wanted her to go. His name on her lips was pulsing incredible sensations through his bloodstream.

Her hands tightened in his. Her hips twitched and her thighs tightened. He could sense her shimmering.

He smiled and whispered her name, urging her over the edge. Then he felt her slide, and he gave in himself, and pure, pristine pleasure cascaded like a waterfall around them.

When it finally stopped, the world filtered through.

The fan whooshed above them, puffing tepid air.

The colorful room came into focus.

Julia's breathing sounded long and deep, her bare breasts rising and falling against his slick chest.

He shifted to remove his weight from her.

"Did I hurt you?" he asked, smoothing stray wisps of hair from her cheek, impulsively kissing the space afterward.

"You suppose it was the adrenaline?" she ventured, gazing straight up at the rotating fan.

He didn't know how to answer that.

He didn't think they could blame the adrenaline.

"Because," she continued, still obviously searching for an explanation, "we don't really like each other all that much."

"We seem to connect on some level," he pointed out.

"I suppose."

Okay, maybe it was ego, but he had to know if he'd been alone in that.

He raised his head on his elbow, gazing down at her. "I mean, have you ever…"

She looked at him. "Had sex?"

He shook his head. "Had sex like *that.*"

"You mean in French?"

He cringed. "I didn't realize you spoke French."

She grinned at his discomfort. "No kidding."

He couldn't even remember all he'd said.

"You're not going to tell me you just had the most incredibly mind-blowing experience of your life, are you?"

"Are you the kind of guy who needs to hear that?"

Her words were tough, but her expression was guarded. He realized that even if they had both felt it, he needed to let the subject drop. Sex alone was complication enough. Sex that might mean something in these circumstances couldn't even be contemplated.

"It must have been the adrenaline," he agreed.

Then they stared at each other for a moment of pure, unadulterated understanding. Adrenaline had had nothing to do with it.

Chapter Ten

Brittany stared in shock at the dozens, no, hundreds, of children and families shrieking, eating or simply running their way around the Wild Wadi Water Park.

"I don't understand," she said to Alex, clutching his arm for support as two ten-year-old boys whipped past her, dripping wet.

"We're hiding in the crowd."

"Why *this* crowd?"

"I thought you were a preschool teacher?"

"It's a private preschool. I have eight students, and they wear uniforms."

Alex grinned. "You don't take them to the park or the zoo?"

"There's a garden in the courtyard of the school."

"Let me guess, where they all play dignified little games in their dignified little uniforms."

Brittany compressed her lips. There was no point in engaging in that particular argument. If Alex thought children could only have fun by racing around like hooligans, that was his problem.

"Do you actually believe the police are following us?" she asked.

"I'm hoping they're following Harrison's money trail." He extracted a credit card from his pocket and waved it in front of her face.

A family came by, two parents, three young children and a baby in arms, screaming its head off.

"Is there any particular reason we can't spend his money somewhere else?"

Alex tugged her in the direction of a shop. "We're here already. Let's pick up some suits and try to have a good time."

"I can assure you, that is not going to happen."

"Not if you don't yank that big ol' stick out of your butt."

Brittany refrained from stating the obvious.

"It's a metaphor," Alex offered helpfully.

"I *know* it's a metaphor. And a rather crude one at that."

"Don't get all prissy on me."

"I am not—" She stopped herself. Arguing with Alex was an exercise in futility. She'd already learned that, and she didn't know why she let herself get drawn in time after time.

"Bathing suits," said Alex, pointing to the display window. "I'll buy you anything you want."

"You mean Harrison will buy me anything I want."

Alex shrugged as he held open the door. "I'm not a very literal guy. So shoot me."

Brittany twitched a grin as she passed him.

"Made-you-laugh time."

"I wasn't laughing at your joke. I was wishing I could take shooting you literally."

He followed her into the brightly lit store. "You were not."

"You don't know what I'm thinking," she said.

He nabbed a bathing suit from the first rack they came to, turning to hold up a bright-green bikini with a halter tie and flirty, little, white bows at the hips. "Want me to tell you what you're thinking?"

She stared at his mocking expression, then she took in the little bikini. It was about her size. Did she dare? It would serve him bloody well right.

He opened his mouth, but she scooped it from his hands. "Perfect. I'll take it."

She was rewarded with a drop of his jaw.

But he recovered quickly. "You're bluffing."

She spotted a matching cover-up and headed for the dressing room. Knew what she was thinking? Ha.

Well, in fact, he'd probably made a pretty decent guess at what she was thinking, which was "not with a gun to my head." But sometimes a girl had to do the unexpected.

She stripped out of the simple, linen dress she'd purchased at the hotel this morning, removed her underwear, and slipped into the bright-green number. The hours spent at the spa's tanning salon had turned her skin a light butternut. And the green and white went well with her blond hair, if she did say so herself.

A little shiver went through her when she thought about Alex's reaction. It was satisfaction, she told herself, not sexual awareness. She shrugged into the sheer cover-up and decided her low-heeled white sandals would work.

Gathering up her clothes and her purse, she exited the dressing room. Alex wasn't around, so she browsed through a rack of tote bags until she found one that coordinated with the outfit, then she packed her clothes into it.

"I'd have bet money against you wearing it," came Alex's deep voice.

Dressed in a pair of tan trunks and a short-sleeved, khaki cotton shirt, he walked around her.

She refused to flinch, even when he paused at the open cover-up, taking in her smooth, bare stomach. The suit bottom rode low, but not indecently so. And the top showed off her cleavage—after all, it was a bikini. And she knew when she took off the cover-up, he was going to see more of her hips than she normally flashed, but there was absolutely no way she was backing down now.

"Nice," he said.

"You better be talking about the bathing suit."

"Why?"

"I'm practically engaged."

"He hasn't asked you yet, sweetheart."

Brittany wanted to disagree, but she realized Alex was technically right, and arguing the point would be wholly undignified.

He relieved her of the tote bag and headed for the cash register. "You bite your tongue a lot, don't you?"

"Only around you."

He tossed a grin over his shoulder. "Really?"

Brittany nodded, realizing how very true the statement was. She rarely argued with people. Well, more to the point, people rarely argued with her.

Which got her to thinking, as she handed the salesclerk the tags from the bikini, was Alex an anomaly, or had the men in her life treated her with kid gloves? Perhaps they hadn't all agreed with her. Perhaps they had contrary opinions that they'd been too polite to share.

Now, there was a humbling thought.

Not Harrison, of course. She and Harrison saw eye to eye on most of the fundamental issues in life. They shared interests in music and art. They attended the same church, were in a similar spot on the political spectrum, had friends in common and enjoyed the same sports.

At least with Harrison, she knew he wasn't putting up a front.

Alex finished the transaction.

Then they stowed their gear in a locker. Alex was all for trying the master blaster, but Brittany held out for one of the gentler slides.

On the climb up the stairs, Alex fell behind.

"Your legs okay?" he asked, catching up again.

"Are you actually inspecting my inner thighs?"

He grinned unrepentantly. "The saddle?"

"Yes. But they're getting better." She ordered herself not to feel self-conscious about the pink spots.

Alex dropped back again.

"Are you out of shape," she called back to him. "Or are you checking out my butt?"

"What do you think?"

"Back up here, sailor." But she couldn't help hoping he liked what he saw. In fact, she hoped he craved and coveted what he saw, and he could wallow in the knowledge he'd never have it.

She realized she was being both conceited and churlish. But she didn't care. If he was going to tease her at every turn, he deserved everything he got.

They made it to the top of the steps, and she gazed at the gush of water racing down the slide.

It was steeper than she'd expected, and she slowed to a stop. She wasn't exactly afraid of heights, but she did have a healthy respect for their ability to cause catastrophic injury.

The slide was long.

And it was very steep.

And the squealing children jumping into the rings and sliding down it apparently had a death wish.

Alex came right up behind her, peering over her shoulder. "What?"

She shook her head.

"Are you scared?"

Heck, *yes,* she was scared. "Maybe."

"Really?"

She shot him a look. She really didn't need his attitude at the moment.

"Then we'll go together," he offered with unexpected kindness. "You're going to love this."

A few others were going down in double tubes, mostly adults and small children.

Okay, small children were also hopping into rubber tubes by themselves and streaking down that flimsy, slippery, scary—

She tried to take a step back, but she bumped into the wall of Alex's bare chest. The contact distracted her for a second. The man was definitely *not* out of shape.

"It'll be fun," he promised.

"Have you done this before?"

"Not here. But back home. As a kid."

"Was that a dig?"

"Not at all. You can do it, Brittany." He took her hand.

His grip was strong, and a funny feeling invaded her stomach. When she looked into his eyes, she wasn't quite as frightened.

"If I die…" she warned him in a dire voice.

He grinned and urged her over to the edge, where an attendant held a double tube.

Not giving herself a chance to change her mind, she clambered into the front. Alex hopped in back.

She closed her eyes, and they pushed off. Cool water splashed them, and her stomach plummeted with the drop.

Alex gave a whoop of delight.

"Do you have your eyes open?" he laughed.

She shook her head.

He leaned forward and placed a wet hand on her shoulder. "Open your eyes," he said more gently. "Come on."

She opened one.

Water splashed over the bow, and she scrunched it shut again.

He shifted in the tube to put his cheek against hers. "You can do it."

She focused on the strength of his hand, his arm, his body. She slowly squinted both eyes open.

They weren't moving as fast as she'd feared. The sides of the ride seemed relatively high. And they were pretty much sticking to the middle of the channel.

"We're halfway," Alex informed her.

She glanced around at the palm trees, the foliage and the colorful people in the ponds and rides around them. Then she glanced down at herself. The combination of her bikini and her sprawled position in the tube was downright provocative. And then she realized Alex was staring over her shoulder and looking at exactly the same thing.

An unfamiliar, prickly flush came over her skin. She should want to move. She should care that he was staring. She should care about what he must be thinking.

But she didn't. It gave her a heady sense of power that had nothing to do with revenge for his teasing.

Then they splashed into the palm-decorated pond at the end of the ride.

"You did great," Alex rumbled, as an attendant slowed their tube.

Alex hopped out, then helped Brittany get to her feet in the shallow pond.

"You want to do that again?" he asked, without letting go of her hand.

Yes, she wanted to do it again.

She wanted very much to have Alex's arm around her bare shoulders, his gaze on her body, his gravelly voice in her ear for another ride down the slide.

It was a little tacky, and probably foolish.

"Earth to Brittany."

"Sure."

"That a girl!"

They splashed their way down a number of the gentler slides. Then they attempted surfing in the flowriders pool. Alex succeeded, but Brittany failed miserably. So instead, they played in the wave pool on some of the tamer toys.

Finally, growing tired, they climbed into an inflatable ring for a lazy ride down the river that wound through the park. They drifted under bridges and beneath the shade of sprawling trees, gazing at the blue sky, and groups of people on shore, who looked worn-out at the end of the day.

"Did you have fun?" asked Alex as the current carried them around a curve, into a quiet, lushly forested area of the park.

"You know I did."

She'd quickly turned into one of the squealing, grinning kamikaze riders.

"You get to do things like this back home?"

She shook her head. Back in London, there were fun days, of course. But there was also her job. And there were a lot of duty days in between. Her family was involved in numerous charities, so there were gallery openings, balls, luncheons, speaking engagements and planning, lots of planning.

She trailed her fingertips in the river water. "My job is only part-time. But I also represent the family."

"Represent the family? That could mean anything."

"We support a lot of charities. I plan parties, dress up, give speeches, write letters, travel." For some reason, her life didn't seem all that exciting at the moment.

"How *do* you cope," he drawled.

"Are you trying to ruin a perfectly nice day?"

His expression turned completely serious. "Do you like it?"

"I…" Yes. She liked it. Did she love it was more to the point. She couldn't think of anything she'd rather do. Then again, she'd never really done anything else.

"Sometimes it's great," she said to Alex. "Often it's boring. Last week, I had lunch with the Royal Ornithological Society for a celebration of the yellow hooded oriole."

Alex quirked a grin.

"They had slides, many, many slides on the various scientific theories of evolution and species habitat."

"But you're not an ornithologist."

"I'm not an ornithologist." Meaning a lot of it was less than thrilling from her perspective. "I've studied art, education, geography and politics," she said.

"Training for the family job," he guessed.

"Pretty much."

"And the preschool thing?"

"I love children."

"Really?" There was skepticism in his tone.

"You doubt me?"

"It sounds like training for a royal mother."

She didn't have the energy to lie. "I expected to get married and have children," she admitted.

"To Harrison."

She shifted in the floating tube, not wanting to open up that topic for Alex's scrutiny. "Let's talk about you."

"You already know I'm a lawyer."

"And a soldier, and a pilot. So what do you do for Harrison?"

"Honestly?" he laughed. "Mostly, I dress up, give speeches, write letters and travel."

Brittany lifted her hands in mock amazement. "We have the same job."

"Only, I suspect my speeches and letters are a lot nastier than yours."

"That's because you're an inherently nastier person."

"Where you're good and kind and compassionate?"

"Exactly."

"You are not."

She matched his light tone. "Are you accusing me of lying, Mr. Lindley?"

He shifted closer. "You, Lady Livingston, are a seething, boiling, repressed cauldron of rebellion."

"Against whom?"

He shrugged. "I don't know yet. Your family—"

"I love my family."

"The constraints of the upper class?"

"Those constraints come with a lot of perks."

"Your duty?"

"I've never resented the obligations that come with privilege."

"Then how about yourself?"

She stared at him in confusion.

"That's it, isn't it?"

"You can't rebel against yourself."

He nodded, straightening as they bobbed their way under another bridge. "That's it. At the top of the first slide, you weren't scared."

"I was so."

He shook his head. "There was something inappropriate and undignified about jumping into an inner tube and shrieking your messy way down a waterslide."

"I was scared," she insisted.

"You have a wall of propriety built up so high and so thick that you're all but screaming to get out. But you won't let yourself out." He sat back with a self-satisfied smile. "You're rebelling against *you*, Lady Livingston. And I really hope you win."

"You have a psychology minor to go along with that law degree?"

"Common sense," he replied.

"What you call a wall, I call etiquette."

"You can't practice good etiquette 24-7."

"The world would be a better place if we did."

His lids grew heavy and his eyes went soft. "Sometimes, Brittany, you gotta forget appearances and shriek your way down the waterslide."

"I did." She glanced away, trying hard not to react to the sensuality of that gaze. "There you go. I'm cured."

Julia found herself reacting with amazement to the man who sat opposite her at the dinner table in the main house at Khandi Oasis. This friendly, open, accepting person couldn't possibly be Nuri's brother.

Ahmed had warmly welcomed them to his home, introduced his wife, Habeeba, and his three daughters.

While the outside of his house was plain and modest, bleached white like all of the buildings in the village, inside, Ahmed boasted all the amenities of the Western world. Led by the development in Dubai, he'd explained, the entire UAE was enjoying prosperity.

The colors were bright, the furnishings decidedly California in style, with light woods, rattan and many cushions, while a computer, DVD player and television were discreetly situated in one corner of the main room. The overall effect was cheerful and modern.

"No one has knowledge of the man with no nose," said Ahmed, dipping his lamb kofta into a bowl of yogurt.

"He has a nose," said Julia, and both men glanced at her. "It's only the tip that's missing."

"They have no knowledge," said Ahmed apologetically.

Julia glanced to Harrison, worried they'd mixed up the description.

"What about a phone?" asked Harrison. "It would be helpful to contact Alex Lindley."

Ahmed said something in Arabic to his eldest daughter, and she slipped away from the table.

Harrison nodded his thanks.

"You say the police are involved?" asked Ahmed.

"Somebody designated Julia a person of significance."

"So there are two parties looking for you," said Ahmed.

"So it seems," said Harrison.

Ahmed looked at Julia. "If you go to an airport, the border guards will stop you. If you run across the desert, the man with no nose might capture you." He thoughtfully dipped another kofta in the yogurt. "I think…"

Julia waited, strangely comforted by the compassion in his eyes.

"While we determine a solution," he told her decisively, "you should eat."

She glanced down at her untouched pita bread and hummus.

Ahmed seemed like an intelligent man. And he didn't seem overly concerned about the danger. Maybe it was just a matter of time until they came up with a solution.

In that case, eating made sense.

She lifted the triangle of bread, as Ahmed's daughter Rania arrived with a satellite phone.

Rania handed it to Harrison, and he stood, taking a few steps away to stand in the entryway while he dialed.

"It's not a secure line," Ahmed warned, and Harrison nodded his understanding.

Julia took a sip of the spicy tea and forced down a bite of the thin bread while she waited.

"Alex?" Harrison began. "It's me."

Then he listened.

His eye squinted, and he glanced at Julia.

"No," he said, and his glance veered away.

She took another bite of bread, and another sip of tea.

Whatever news the phone call brought, starving herself wouldn't make it any better.

"Are you sure?" asked Harrison. "No name?"

Another silence, while the entire family watched and waited.

"No. You're right. Thanks." He shut off the phone.

Suddenly, there was a loud banging on the door behind him.

Harrison spun, while Ahmed jumped to his feet.

He issued rapid-fire instructions in Arabic, and Habeeba quickly ushered Julia into a small, window-less bedroom.

Harrison was right behind her, and he closed the door, trapping them in the dark.

"What—"

"Shh," he warned, listening at the door to the cresting voices in the other room. Julia couldn't understand the words, but it was clear the speakers were agitated.

She stood stock-still, all her fears of arrest and jail rushing back. She refused to even acknowledge her fears of the man with no nose. The bites of pita bread sat like lead weights in her stomach.

Then, finally, the voices subsided, and the door to the bedroom cracked open.

"A sandstorm is coming," said Ahmed.

The girls were moving from window to window, battening them down. Ahmed's wife covered her head and left the house.

"Julia," said Ahmed, "you are welcome to stay in the guesthouse with Harrison, of course. But, if you prefer, please stay here and sleep with my daughters."

It was gracious of him to consider Julia's virtue. Not that there was any virtue left to save. And, as she glanced from friendly, cherubic Ahmed to fierce, un-compromising Harrison, she knew where she wanted to be if No-nose showed up.

"Thank you," she said to Ahmed with sincere appre-ciation, trying to frame an answer that wouldn't offend Ahmed's culture. "But Harrison has pledged to protect me. My family is counting on him."

Ahmed nodded. "Very well." Then he looked to Harrison. "You should return to the guesthouse before the storm hits."

Harrison handed the phone back to Ahmed, thank-ing the man.

Then Julia and Harrison left the building, hustling along the dusty pathway to the little cottage.

"Your family is counting on me?" he joked.

"You've probably disappointed them already," she told him, deciding she could be blasé about their earlier lovemaking. It wasn't as though she was a quivering virgin. They'd been attracted to one another, and they'd had sex. It didn't have to be the defining moment of their relationship.

"In some cultures, they'd have me shot."

"In other cultures, they'd invite you to dinner." Julia's feet slowed to a halt, her eyes widening at a gap in the trees.

A thick, dark, roiling wave was pushing its way across the setting sun.

Harrison grabbed her hand. "Time to get inside." He increased his pace, forcing her to struggle to keep up.

She couldn't help but glance back over her shoulder, amazed by the spectacle. The light disappeared, and the wind picked up, flecks of sand whipping through the air.

Harrison yanked open the cottage door, pushed her inside and secured it behind them.

"Check the windows," he called.

She glanced around. The windows were all closed, but she went from one to the next, checking the latches, while airborne sand began battering the outside of the panes.

Then the wind suddenly turned from gusting to howling. The panes rattled in their frames, and she took a few steps backward.

"Will the place hold?" she asked.

"I expect so. This can't be their first sandstorm."

"How long will it last?"

"Hours, days. It's impossible to tell."

They had some time. It was a relief to have some time where they didn't need to worry.

"And then what?" she couldn't help but ask.

He didn't answer immediately.

"What did Alex tell you?"

"That the police are still looking for you, and he can't get an answer as to why."

Julia lowered herself into a cushioned rattan chair. "I don't understand."

"Neither does Alex. But somebody with influence is out there looking for you, and they're using the police to do it." He sat down in an identical chair across from her. "And whoever it is is powerful enough to cover his tracks. Alex's contacts couldn't help us."

"What about the no-nose guy?"

"It all has to be related somehow."

"Which brings us back to Millions to Spare." Julia still got a hitch in her heart when she thought about the horse. She hated that she might have inadvertently contributed to its death.

"What did you say to No-nose?"

She'd gone over the conversation a hundred times in

her head. "Nothing. I tried to take a picture of Millions to Spare. The security guy stopped me. Then No-nose showed up, and I asked him the horse's name. He thought I wanted to place a bet."

"No, he acted like he thought you wanted to place a bet."

Julia went cold. "You think he could have followed me to the trailer?"

Harrison nodded. "And watched you go in. And saw that you didn't get out. Then came to Cadair."

The next sentence was left unspoken.

No-nose had killed Millions to Spare.

Chapter Eleven

"Did Alex have a plan?" asked Julia, standing by the window to watch the mesmerizing sand grains blow past. At least she knew No-nose wasn't lurking out there in the brutal storm.

"Not so far," said Harrison, crouching to browse through the small bank of cupboards in one corner of the twenty-by-twenty-foot room.

"Maybe I should turn myself in." At the moment, No-nose seemed a lot more dangerous than the police. If she was in custody, the U.S. embassy might help her. Maybe Harrison could even help get her out of jail again. She truly didn't want to take her chances with a man who was willing to kill a horse.

"Not until we find out what they want," said Harrison, extracting a butcher knife and contemplating it.

Julia got the horrible feeling he was arming himself.

He straightened. "If the same person influencing the police also hired No-nose, he could be capable of anything. And the police might turn you over to him."

Julia's knees grew weak, and she reached out to steady herself on the back of a chair.

Harrison caught her movement. He set down the knife and crossed the room, pulling her into a hug. She felt safe for a moment, but she knew it couldn't last.

"We'll come up with a plan," he promised.

"Plans fail."

"Are you going to get pessimistic on me?"

"I'm not a pessimist, I'm a realist. There are crazy men out there gunning for me—"

"And there's a sane one in here protecting you."

A lump formed in Julia's throat, and she couldn't speak.

His arms tightened around her, and she rested her cheek against his broad chest, closing her eyes for a moment.

He gently kissed the top of her head.

"I know you're scared," he said. "But we have a very long list of options that we haven't even tried yet."

Part of her wanted to ask what the options were. Another part was afraid they were laughably weak. Maybe it was better to pretend Harrison had a long list of rational courses of action that would save her. Denial might not be such a bad thing in this case.

"We should sleep," he said.

"I know." They'd been up virtually all night, and she was dead tired. "You should sleep, too."

"There's only one bed," he pointed out.

She glanced at the colorful jumble of blankets and pillows. "It seems a little silly for me to go all Victorian on you now."

He kissed her hair again and pulled back to smile. "There are things about you I like very much, Julia Nash."

"There are things about you I like very much, too." Specifically, at the moment, she liked that he felt like a barrier between her and the world.

He turned off the light above the cupboards.

Ahmed had thoughtfully provided Julia with a plain, white cotton nightgown, so she slipped into the tiny bathroom to wash up and change.

When she came out, a single light glowed next to the bed, the sand was invisible where it rattled against the dark windows, and the ceiling fan turned lazily above.

As she padded across the room to the small bed, she could feel Harrison's gaze on her. But without looking in his direction, she lay down, tucked her head against a pillow and pulled up a single, thin sheet.

She heard him cross the room.

A rustle as he discarded his clothes.

She assumed—*hoped*—he slept in his boxers as he lifted the sheet to join her.

The bed was too small to stay away from each other. And, after a minute or so of hopeless attempts to find a politically correct position to sleep in, Harrison wrapped his arm around her waist and pulled her, spoon style, against his body.

It seemed to her that she should argue. But then, she felt safe and comfortable in his arms, and it wasn't as if they hadn't already touched every inch of each other that could possibly be touched. So, instead of putting up a fight, she relaxed against him.

He rested his chin against her hair, and his hand grew warm where it splayed across her belly. She could have easily turned in his arms, easily kissed him, touched him, made love with him all over again.

"Can we talk about Brittany?" she braved.

He drew a breath. "I really don't know what to say about Brittany."

"I feel like the other woman."

"I'm not with Brittany yet."

Yet being the operative word. But Julia didn't say that out loud.

"You're *before* Brittany," said Harrison with conviction. "Not at the same time as Brittany."

He was obviously trying to make both of them feel better. On one level, it worked. On another, it made Julia sad. Harrison had a destiny with Brittany. He was simply biding his time with Julia.

Her chest tightened in pain. Then she told herself to buck up. She and Harrison had been thrown together in an artificial situation. Their emotions were magnified. Neither of them was even thinking clearly.

When it was over, they'd go back to their regular lives, and this would all be a fond, or maybe a frightening memory—depending on how things turned out.

But, for now, she had to focus on the moment. And, at the moment, Harrison was helping her. He said he had options, and she was going to believe him.

And *that* was all that mattered.

With Julia sleeping in his arms, Harrison tried to conceive a plan to get her safely out of UAE. Unfortunately, her warm skin, her sweet scent and especially her soft bottom pressing against him were more than a little distracting.

The storm had settled into a steady hum outside.

They were safe for now, but as soon as the storm passed, they ran the risk of being discovered.

He redoubled his efforts to focus on something other than his desire to make love with her all over again.

He could rent a helicopter. But even if the police hadn't put the airlines on alert, they ran the risk of being shot down if they tried to cross the border without clearance. Same problem with driving across a border; they could easily run into a patrol. And, even if they made it into Oman or Saudi Arabia, they might find more trouble there than they'd left behind.

He could take her south to the coastal town of Ruwais, find a boat of some kind and make the short crossing to Qatar. He turned that approach over in his mind. It was probably their best bet. But he'd have to get her there. And he didn't dare make arrangements over the airwaves. They'd have to take their chances on finding a willing captain once they got to the town.

Mind made up, he realized he needed to sleep. It might be his last chance for a while. He'd ask Ahmed for a gun in the morning, pack as much fuel and water as the Jeep would carry, and make a run down the back roads of the desert past the dead zone.

He gathered Julia close, wrapping his body protectively around her as his eyes fluttered closed.

He woke up with a start, arms automatically tightening around her. The storm had passed, and the village was eerily quiet.

And then he heard it.

The sound of a diesel truck.

Carefully extracting his arm from beneath her, and his leg from where he'd thrown it over her hip in the night, he slipped out of bed. He crossed to the window, and cautiously peeked out. The engine sound grew louder as the driver geared down, and Harrison realized it had to be a semi. Probably not a threat then.

A tanker truck came into view on the main road of the oasis, then it passed behind a building and kept going. Harrison took a precautionary glance around the village before returning to the bed.

Julia's eyes were open and wary.

"Everything okay?" she whispered.

Harrison nodded. "But we should get moving."

She pulled herself into a sitting position. "Where are we going?"

"Ruwais. It's a small town in the south. We can get a boat to Qatar."

"What about the border?"

"It'll look like we're taking a day trip when we leave. To the authorities in Qatar, we'll look like a couple of Western tourists."

Julia smiled, and the glow of gratitude in her eyes did something to his stomach.

"Get dressed," he advised, hoping she'd do it quickly, before he said or did something really stupid. "I'm going to pack a few things in the Jeep."

She scooted out of bed, and he had to force himself to drag his gaze from the thin cotton that molded itself to her body as she moved. She was naked under there, and he remembered exactly what a sweet sight that was.

"Do you need any help?" she asked on her way to the bathroom.

"Ahmed will have breakfast for us. Could you pack it up? Then we can eat on the road."

She nodded, pausing with the door half-closed. "Thank you."

"Anytime." And he meant it.

As the door clicked shut behind her, he realized just how much he was willing to do for her, and how often he was willing to do it.

He pulled on the loose, cotton pants and shirt Ahmed had provided, then slipped his feet into the sturdy sandals. No point heading out into the desert in his wingtips.

He waited until Julia was ready, then he escorted her to the main house, watching carefully around them as he went.

Ahmed was up, as was the rest of the family. And, as Harrison had predicted, a breakfast of fruit, breads, cheese and strong coffee was laid out on the table.

Harrison gratefully accepted a cup of the coffee, then asked Ahmed if he had a weapon available.

Ahmed drew him aside.

"You'll need more than a handgun," he said in a low tone, glancing toward the women.

"Do you know something?" asked Harrison, turning his back, but feeling Julia's stare on him.

"The man with no nose."

Harrison raised his eyebrows.

"He is Muwaffaq. And he has connections."

Organized crime? "To whom?"

"I don't know yet."

Harrison clenched his jaw. This was definitely a bigger problem than he'd expected. "Do you have any idea what he wants?"

Ahmed shook his head.

"Harrison?" Julia appeared at his elbow.

Ahmed looked startled by the interruption. He might be a thoroughly modern Arab man, but he was still an Arab man, unused to women as complete equals.

"What's going on?" she asked.

"We're just about ready to go," said Harrison, deciding there was no advantage in worrying her any further.

"Go?" asked Ahmed.

"To Ruwais," said Harrison. "We'll get a boat from there."

"To *Ruwais?*" Ahmed gave Harrison a look that clearly questioned his sanity.

"We'll take extra fuel," said Harrison.

"You can't cross the desert."

Harrison gave Ahmed a hard look.

"Why not?" asked Julia.

"Muwaffaq is raising a mob to chase you."

Julia's face blanched. "Muwaffaq?"

"No-nose," Harrison admitted, rebuking Ahmed with his eyes. Ruwais might be a risky move, but it was still the best move.

"A *mob?*"

"You're not helping," Harrison told Ahmed.

"You can't leave," said Ahmed.

"Well, we can't stay," said Harrison. "How long do you think it'll take desert telegraph to let him know we're here?"

Ahmed's gaze darted from Harrison to Julia and back again. "There is another way," he said.

Julia looked eager.

Harrison was listening.

"We arrange a new passport for her."

"Oh, no," said Julia with a shake of her head. "I'm not traveling through the Middle East on a forged passport. That's a *real* crime."

"I wasn't referring to a forgery."

"I'm a U.S. citizen," she said. "My name is Julia Margarite Nash. There's no way you can change that."

"Yes, there is."

Harrison struggled to understand Ahmed's logic. They didn't have nearly enough time to change Julia's name.

Ahmed gave Harrison a searching, speculative look. "We get her a diplomatic passport. From the British High Commission."

Harrison rocked back, words failing him.

"What?" asked Julia, easily picking up on the unspoken tension between the two men.

And then she understood, and her eyes lit with hope. "Ohhh. Your get out of jail free card."

"No way," Harrison barked, and they both blinked at him.

He couldn't get married in a Bedouin settlement in the middle of the Arabian desert. His grandmother would have a heart attack for one.

"It would solve your problem," said Ahmed. "Even if they caught her, they couldn't hold her."

"A marriage certificate is not some cold, utilitarian document you sign to get a good piece of identification."

"We'd get divorced," Julia offered. "Right away if you want."

"There's protocol," said Harrison. "My family."

"Brittany," said Julia with a sigh, the hope going out of her eyes.

"Never mind Brittany. I'm Lord Harrison William—"

"Arthur Beaumont-Rochester, Baron Welsmeire," she finished for him.

"It's not a curse," he told her. "But it is an obligation."

"I understand," said Julia. "Forget about it."

Ahmed compressed his lips, and Harrison could feel the man's disapproval.

"The decision is not mine alone," he tried to explain. Divorce was strongly frowned upon by the royal family and the Church. Harrison could taint his marriage to Brittany, their future children, perhaps even his family's title.

"I said to forget about it," Julia repeated. "We'll find another way."

He opened his mouth to argue again, but then he caught her expression. She wasn't angry or upset. She was genuinely letting him off the hook.

He gave a nod. "Ruwais," he said.

"Suicide," Ahmed muttered under his breath.

Harrison glared at him.

Packing up the Jeep for the run to Ruwais, Julia fought hard to keep her fear at bay. Ahmed must have been exaggerating the danger. Otherwise, Harrison wouldn't be willing to drive her across the desert.

She understood Harrison's position. He had to get married in St. Paul's Cathedral amidst the pomp and circumstance expected of a man of his station. He owed it to Brittany, and he owed it to his family. His behavior had been nothing short of heroic in this, and it was unfair of her to expect more.

The rich lived by a different code of conduct, and she had to accept that reality.

She squelched her disappointment and promised herself everything would be okay. They'd take back roads across the desert. They had plenty of fuel, plenty of water, and food to sustain them on the journey.

They wouldn't have to stop in any towns, so the odds of anyone recognizing them were practically nil. The odds of Muwaffaq running into them on the road again were similarly small. There was no point in ruining Harrison's life when there was another perfectly good option.

He could drop her in Qatar, and she'd make her own way to London. From there, it was a simple flight to any number of cities on the eastern seaboard. She'd be fine.

They got in either side and buckled up. They'd conserve fuel by forgoing the air-conditioning once again. But this time, Julia had light cotton clothes. She'd also brought along a translucent head scarf in case they came across any travelers. She'd draw less attention to herself if her head was covered, and it would help camouflage the fact that she was a Westerner.

The Jeep was packed tight with the supplies they'd need. They also had two spare tires, extra belts and a small tool kit.

Harrison turned the key and started the Jeep.

Julia tightened her ponytail and stared determinedly down the dusty road. Ahmed had described the route to them. It was pretty much due south, though they'd have to eventually veer east. But they'd wait until they were well clear of Abu Dhabi to avoid the increase in traffic around the capital city.

Julia waited for the Jeep to move.

She waited.

She glanced over at Harrison.

His jaw was clenched, and he was staring at some unseen point on the horizon.

She squinted ahead.

He shut off the Jeep.

"What's wrong?" she asked.

He twisted in the bucket seat, crooking his knee around the gearshift. "If we do this…"

If? Weren't they about to leave? Like, right this minute?

"You can't tell a soul."

"Okay," she said slowly. Was he worried about the consequences of transporting a fugitive?

"I mean it. When I get married next year in London, our divorce is between me, you and God."

Divorce?

"And we do it as soon as possible." He pulled the key from the ignition and reached for the door handle.

"Wait!" She grabbed his arm.

"What?"

"Are you saying you changed your mind?" Was he offering to marry her?

"Yes."

"What about Brittany? All that stuff about your family name and obligations?"

"I'm not about to kill you to protect my family name."

"But you can't be—"

"What good is protecting my family name," he continued as if she hadn't even spoken, "if doing so costs me my family honor?"

"You don't have to do this, Harrison."

It was a grand gesture. It was an amazing gesture. But the odds of success were with them. They could drive through the desert and accomplish exactly the same thing, without screwing up his life.

"Yes, I do," he said.

"No, you—"

"Yes." His tone was implacable. "Ahmed is right. I marry you, and you're home free."

"But you're not."

"I'll manage."

"Harrison."

"I said I would manage."

"I won't let you do this."

His dark eyes became uncompromising. "You're in the Middle East, Julia. A willing bride is not a prerequisite to a successful wedding."

She felt her spine stiffen. "You wouldn't."

He opened the door to the Jeep. "Watch me."

Chapter Twelve

Curled up in a corner of her Emirates Palace hotel room in Abu Dhabi, Brittany watched the early-morning waves roll in on the white sand beach of the peninsula. There was a storm brewing out there somewhere, because the wind whipped the palm fronds, and white foam sparkled under the rising sun.

As they had the past two nights, Alex and Brittany had checked into one hotel with Harrison's credit card, then stayed in a second one using cash. There was no way to know if the police were still following them, but they'd try to give Harrison a few more days to get Julia out of the country before they returned to Cadair.

After that, well, it was back to normal life.

Brittany was experiencing increasingly conflicted emotions about that. She wanted Harrison to propose— what woman wouldn't? But there was something about

Alex, something she had to deal with, something that called to her on an untamed, sensual level.

They'd danced the night away at the Emirates Palace club last night. And, for what was probably the first time in her life, she'd been completely uninhibited on the dance floor. In London, and on official trips with her family, there was always the danger of reporters snapping a picture and writing an unflattering story.

But, last night, in a crowded club, deep in Abu Dhabi, with an anonymous, American lawyer, she'd known the dancing was only about the moment. And it had been brilliant.

A soft knock came at her door, and she rose in the white, embroidered robe. It had been less than ten minutes since she'd called room service for coffee and pastries—just another example of the hotel's impeccable service.

But when she opened the door, it was Alex, looking sexy and casual in a white, mandarin-collared shirt and lightweight black slacks.

"I didn't want to call and wake you," he said.

"Coffee's on the way." She stood back to let him in.

"You feeling okay this morning?"

It had been 3:00 a.m. before they'd called it quits last night. A combination of adrenaline, tropical cocktails and, in her case, runaway hormones had kept them lively through the late night. They'd finally ended with a jazzy waltz beneath the lighted palm trees by the hotel's west pool, where, for a second, she'd thought Alex was going to kiss her.

But he didn't.

"I'm fine," she told him now. And she was. Her short sleep had been deep and satisfying.

He smiled down at her as he entered the hallway, voice going low. "Have a good time last night?"

"I did."

"Different than your regular balls?"

"A little," she allowed, as the door swung shut behind him.

He waited for her to move, then followed her through the entryway to the cozy set of ice-blue chairs clustered around the wide, arched window.

She sat down, arranging the delicate robe around her legs, half tempted to let it fall open.

Was he attracted to her? He'd seen her in a bikini yesterday and in a slim, little black party dress last night. Fundamentally, he'd behaved like a gentleman throughout. But, every once in a while, she thought she caught a flare of heat in his eyes.

She'd caught more than a few unaccustomed flares of heat in her own body. Alex was an incredibly attractive man, one of those men who looked better and better as you got to know them and they let you see their range of intelligence and emotion. He was also very different from the men she'd met in her past.

Sometime last night, she'd realized the difference was that he didn't care about impressing her. After a lifetime of fawning gentlemen, there was something exciting about the one who did whatever the heck he wanted, whether she approved or not. Which, in a strange way, gave her permission to do the same thing.

So she let the robe fall open, showing off most of her right leg. Then she curled her feet beneath her on the wide, soft chair, not even caring that the position nearly exposed her bare hip. There was something exhilarat-

ing about the pose, and something even more exhilarating about Alex's avid gaze.

He stared at the smooth, softly tanned leg. "You
know," he began in a quiet voice, "you are not what
Harrison thinks you are."

Okay, she'd bite. "What does Harrison think I am?"

Alex's attention moved to her eyes. "Some decorative
appendage without a mind of her own." He sat forward
in his chair, taking in the complete length of her body.
"You, sweetheart, definitely have a mind of your own."

"And that's a bad thing?" She shifted, and the robe
inched up.

He reached across the space between them. Then he
traced his fingertip from her midthigh, over her knee
and down her calf.

Her muscles contracted and her breath caught.

"This work often?" he asked mildly, lifting his finger
from her ankle.

She wasn't exactly sure what he meant.

He looked into her eyes. "For getting men into your
bed."

"I've never had a man in my bed."

The second the words were out, she realized what
she'd admitted.

Alex squinted. Then he rocked back. "Come again?"

She didn't know what to say.

"Brittany?"

"Too much information?"

"How *old* are you?"

Her embarrassment quickly turned to annoyance. It
was hardly a crime to be a virgin. "I'm twenty-five."

"Yet, you've never…" He lifted his hands in a
gesture of confusion. "You're stunning as sin. You prac-

tically killed me on the dance floor last night. And that bikini would get you on the cover of any magazine in the world. How on earth…"

What? She was supposed to take every offer that came her way?

"There are two kinds of men in my life," she told him bluntly. "The kind that are afraid of my father, and the kind that would run to the tabloids. Who was I supposed to sleep with? Tell me?"

"For the record," he said, "I picked up the ball on your little seduction there, because I thought you knew what you were doing."

"I've been sleeping in my own bed," she countered. "Not hiding under a rock. I knew exactly what I was doing."

"I can't sleep with you, Brittany."

"Why not?" Okay, that hadn't come out exactly as she'd planned. She might be inexperienced, but bitchy and demanding didn't seem like a particularly effective seduction technique.

She wasn't sure exactly when she'd decided to seduce Alex. She wasn't in a hurry to lose her virginity, and she certainly wasn't desperate. It was just that he was Alex. And there was something about him. And she knew if she didn't do this she'd spend the rest of her life wondering.

"One word," he said in answer to her terse question.

She waited.

"Harrison."

"Do you honestly believe Harrison will care if I'm not a virgin on our wedding night?"

"Harrison will care *very much* that it was me."

"Oh." She hadn't thought about that.

"Yeah."

"He'd fire you?"

"I'd quit."

Okay, that wasn't good. She tucked her leg beneath the robe where it belonged. "Guess I'd better go back to repressing."

"That would be good."

She bobbed her head for a moment. "Too bad. I kind of liked having a wild side."

"You could turn Harrison down."

"And have a fling with you?"

"And do anything you want. Just because you're programmed to find a titled husband doesn't mean you—"

"Programmed?"

"What would you call it?"

"Harrison and I have many things in common."

"Like money, titles and property holdings?"

"Like religion, politics, art and mutual friends."

"Are you in love with him?"

"He's a lovable man."

"Does he make your heart beat faster, your skin prickle with heat, your toes curl?"

That wasn't a fair question. Those things made for a good fling, not a good marriage. Marriage was more than mere physical attraction.

"Because, if he doesn't, sweetheart," Alex drawled, "it's going to be a bloody long marriage."

She pulled herself forward in the chair. "Why do you care?"

The question seemed to stop him. Seconds ticked by. "I don't know," he finally said.

"Are you protecting Harrison?" she asked. "Are you afraid I'll make him a bad wife?"

Alex's gaze dropped to where her robe gaped open.

At the touch of his gaze, her heart beat faster, and her skin prickled with heat.

"No," he finally said in a voice that was low and tight with emotion. "I'm afraid I'll have to quit my job anyway, because I won't be able to stand watching the two of you together."

Brittany's heart thudded deep and hollow. She could swear she heard it through the silence that boomed in the room.

"So," he breathed and rose to his feet, his eyes focused on the cleavage revealed by the robe. "I guess, since that's the case, I'm in. Your call."

She slowly rose to face him. Could she sleep with Alex then marry Harrison? It was what she wanted, but she couldn't shake the sense of betrayal. Ironically, though, it seemed like a betrayal of Alex rather than of Harrison.

"I can't," she managed.

Alex smiled, reaching out to gently stroke her cheek with the pad of his thumb. "Of course you can't."

"But I want to." She owed him her honesty, at least.

He cupped her cheek. "So do I."

She closed her eyes and rested against his open hand, its warmth bittersweet. Her own hand rose to his wrist, wrapping around its thick strength and holding on, desperately afraid to let go of the moment.

He took a step forward, smoothing her hair with his other hand. She inhaled the hiss of his breath, subconsciously leaning into his scent and his strength.

Then his lips touched hers, and hot emotion swamped her, cresting along her limbs, flushing her skin.

She kissed him back, and the world fell away.

He opened his mouth, and his hand slipped around, anchoring at the back of her neck, holding her close while he kissed her thoroughly, deeply, expertly.

She took her own step forward, bringing their bodies together, and his arm went around her waist, while hers snaked around his neck. The knot in her sash rubbed free. Her robe slipped open. And his raw cotton shirt abraded her tender skin.

Sparks of desire shot down her spine. Want pooled in her belly, and need softened her bones, making it difficult to stand.

Alex's lips left her mouth. They trailed down her cheek to the crook of her neck, to the tip of her shoulder, pushing the flimsy robe until it slipped down her arm. He pushed the other side, and the fabric whispered down to pool at her feet.

He drew back to look, eyes dark with desire.

He groaned once, then scooped her into his arms and crossed to the bed.

The air whispered over her bare skin. His hands were hard and solid against her. His arms were strong, his body sturdy. She wasn't engaged, and they were both adults, and they were perfectly free to make this decision.

He laid her down, then straightened away, his eyes determined and defiant as he worked his way down the buttons of his shirt. She watched him, mesmerized as he stripped it off. His chest was impressive, dark and broad, sculpted with muscles that corded into his shoulders and neck.

His hands moved to his slacks, popping the button, drawing down on the zipper.

The room air was cool, but his gaze was hot. It

traveled the length of her body then back again. Need roared in her ears, and it clouded her brain, until all she could see was a tall, naked, god of a man sinking down on the bed beside her. His hand closed over her breast. His mouth met her swollen lips. And his thigh slid up between hers, landing solid, sending rivers of sensation straight up to her brain.

His thumb rasped her nipple, and she reflexively arched. He murmured soothing words, gentling the caress.

She stroked his arms, clasped his shoulders, kissed his lips and tangled with his tongue.

After that, she was lost.

"What do I do?" Her whisper was pained against his mouth.

"Anything you want." He kissed her again. "Trust me, it won't be wrong."

His hand slid down her rib cage, cupping her bottom, kneading the soft flesh.

She feathered her fingertips down his chest, feeling the hot play of his muscles, the sparse hair, his flat nipples.

He sucked in a breath, so she tried it again, smiling to herself when she realized he liked it. She swirled down lower, and lower still.

He gasped. "You want this to be over quick?"

"I have no idea."

"Trust me, you don't." He retrieved her hands, putting them safely against his back.

But when his wandered to her thighs, she copied his movements. They stared at each other, alternately kissing and touching and teasing, as their bodies grew slick and the tension ratcheted up between them.

Then finally, he trapped her wrists in one hand, holding them out of harm's way. He gently urged her thighs apart, watching her expression as he positioned himself above her.

Her breathing was laboured, her skin itchy hot, her limbs and her body twitchy with need. He touched against her, and her eyes went wide. Her lips went soft and she leaned up to kiss his mouth.

Her hips flexed, and her thighs quivered.

"Now," she pleaded.

"I can't believe—" He pressed against her.

She groaned and arched and freed her hands to wrap her arms around his neck.

"I can't believe," he repeated, "that I'm about to ruin both our lives."

Then he flexed, and she gasped, and his solid thickness filled her. Heat instantly pulsed where their bodies joined.

She brought up her knees, and sharp pain was replaced by swirling desire.

"You okay?" he gasped, even as his body moved in its own rhythm.

"Don't…" she groaned back. "Stop…" She sucked in a breath. "Ruining my life."

"Brittany." His hand slipped beneath her buttocks, refining their angle. "I could ruin your life forever."

Events had quickly spiralled out of Julia's control. Although there was a serious language barrier, the thrill of a wedding seemed universal. Ahmed's wife, Habeeba, had immediately begun issuing orders, while the oldest daughter, Rania, pulled Julia into one of the bedrooms.

She laughed and gestured for Julia to sit on a small chair in front of a gilt, oval mirror. When she began combing Julia's hair, Julia quickly realized she was being prepared to be a bride. She wanted to protest that it was unnecessary, but Rania seemed so excited that she didn't have the heart to stop her.

Rania smoothed Julia's hair back into a flat braid. Then she offered her a warm cloth and gestured for her to wash her face. Julia smiled and nodded, trying to express her appreciation without words.

She didn't know what Harrison was doing outside, but she hoped it was more along the lines of getting the local marriage official and filling out the paperwork.

She was far from convinced this was a good idea. But if they were going to do it, they'd better get it done and get out of here.

She had no doubt Muwaffaq was scouring the desert for them, and she doubted he'd stop to ask for their passports.

Chatting as she worked, not seeming the least bit concerned that Julia didn't understand her, Rania carefully applied cosmetics to Julia's freshly washed face. She brushed and blended, and stroked the subtle colors onto Julia's eyes, lips and cheeks.

Then, apparently satisfied, she pulled over another small, wooden chair and reached for Julia's hands. As she began washing them, Julia forced out another smile. She didn't really need a manicure. A preacher alone would do the trick.

She surreptitiously glanced behind her.

Where *was* Harrison?

Then, the bedroom door opened. But Julia's sigh of relief was short-lived. Instead of Harrison come to rescue her, she saw Habeeba coming through the door. The woman carried a small, ceramic bowl and a hand towel.

She spoke to Rania, who stood up and relieved her mother of the bowl.

Then Habeeba sat down across from Julia and reached for her hands. Before Julia knew what was happening, the older woman had dipped a brush into the dark paste in the bowl and started to draw on the back of Julia's hand.

Julia fought an instinct to snatch her hand away. But, quickly, an intricate design of scrolls and flowers appeared. Rania and her mother chatted to Julia and with each other, with Rania pointing and commenting as the drawing took shape.

Julia got that it was some kind of wedding tradition. She also realized the paste must be made from henna dye.

The talking and painting went on and on. When the older woman finally finished her hands, Julia breathed a sigh of relief. But Rania immediately went to work on her feet. A good hour later, they finished off with a small pattern at the base of her neck.

Finally satisfied, they motioned for Julia to hold still and let the dye dry. They brought her a snack of bread and yogurt, with tea to wash it down.

Habeeba then returned to the kitchen, while Rania began organizing colorful clothing and fabrics.

"Harrison?" Julia finally forced herself to ask, afraid of moving for fear of ruining their designs, but growing more desperate to know what was going on outside.

Rania made a frantic negative gesture with her head and hands.

Julia sighed.

Obviously, there was no seeing the groom before the ceremony. It was amazing how many customs transcended cultures.

Finally, it was time to wash the henna paste off with water. Then Rania helped her dress in a brightly patterned tunic in burgundy, white and coral blue. They adorned her neck, ears and wrists with heavy gold, then added an intricately embroidered head scarf, woven with gold and silver threads and draped to cover the lower half of her face.

She gazed at her exotic image in the small mirror, then down at hands that seemed to belong to someone else. Despite the knowledge she'd have to hide this secret forever, she began to hope somebody out there had a camera.

Rania touched her arm. With a smile, the young woman nodded toward the bedroom door. Julia understood.

It was time.

Suddenly nervous, trying to keep it all in perspective, and hoping the sweat on her palms wouldn't make the henna run, she started for the door.

Exotic, half-tone string music was playing in the main room, and they entered to see Ahmed and Habeeba, their two other daughters and a man who was obviously the marriage official standing in the middle of the room. The women were dressed in bright colors, the men in crisp whites. Then she caught sight of Harrison. He smiled reassuringly, dressed in a simple white cap, a bright white tunic and matching trousers.

Not sure what to do, Julia stood with the women on one side of the room while the preacher began speaking. She didn't understand a word of what was said. And when the man stopped talking, Harrison didn't kiss her. Instead he motioned for her to join him at the table.

She didn't feel married. Which was a relief, really. Walking down some kind of aisle in a white dress and repeating vows she wouldn't keep would have been much worse than this foreign ceremony and the Arabic certificate in front of her.

"This could be anything," she said, sitting down to pick up the pen.

"It's a prenup."

She shot him a look of astonishment.

"I'm joking." Then he paused. "But you're not going after Cadair or anything, are you?"

"No."

Harrison's wealth was completely safe from her. Even if she was corrupt enough to try to capitalize on the marriage, she doubted any court would award her a settlement. Besides, the last thing she wanted was to come back and visit the UAE. In fact, it might be a while before she left Kentucky again.

He pointed to a line on the page. She drew a breath, told herself it was nothing but a temporary legal contract, and signed the document. Then Harrison sat down and signed his name, as well.

The small group surrounding them gave a lilting, high-pitched cheer, and Ahmed cranked up the music.

Rania and her sisters immediately began serving food.

"Where's your passport?" Harrison asked Julia, drawing her aside.

Julia pointed to the pouch that hung around her neck, beneath her blouse.

Harrison held out his hand. "I've got a chopper waiting for our ID and the marriage certificate."

"You're taking them away?"

"Ahmed's brother Rafiq will take them to the British High Commission in Abu Dhabi and wait while they issue your diplomatic passport."

Julia drew on the string that held the passport pouch. "They can do that?"

"Yes, they can."

"Are you sure it's safe?" She wasn't too crazy about giving up her passport.

"Nuri made the arrangements."

Julia hesitated. Where Nuri was involved, things didn't seem to go so well for her.

"He has nothing against you," Harrison assured her. "And he's extremely loyal to me."

Julia nodded and extracted the little black book and handed it over. Nuri aside, trusting Harrison's judgment had kept her free and safe this long.

He exited the house, while Rania handed her a cup of mint tea and offered her a stuffed date.

Julia's anxiety was returning in force, and she wasn't particularly hungry, but the family had worked so hard on the impromptu wedding that she didn't want to do anything to offend them. So she accepted both with a smile and a thank-you.

Then Harrison returned to her side.

"How long?" she asked him.

"A couple of hours."

She nodded, her stomach knotting further. A lot could happen in a few hours.

Chapter Thirteen

Two hours later, Harrison breathed a sigh of relief as the returning chopper put down on the sand outside the oasis.

The passenger door opened, and Ahmed's brother hopped out, ducking his head against the rotors and the swirling sand. He quickly crossed to Harrison, handing him a diplomatic pouch.

Harrison shouted his thanks, then signaled for Julia to come out of the small house near the landing site where she had waited with Ahmed. She'd changed into plainer clothes, but her makeup was still heavy, and her hands were patterned with henna dye.

With a quick glance around the town for any danger, he took her hand and they dashed across the sand to the chopper.

Harrison helped her into the backseat, then climbed in next to the pilot and signaled for the man to take off.

Ahmed's family had insisted that Julia keep the wedding jewelry. In return, Harrison had left the keys to the Jeep for Ahmed.

As they pulled toward the blue sky, Harrison broke the seal on the pouch. He extracted Julia's new passport and handed it back to her.

The relief on her face did his heart good. They'd succeeded. She'd be safe now.

She opened the book and looked down at her new name, and a flash of unease went through her eyes. He was reminded she was safe at a cost. He reached back to squeeze her knee.

"It's going to be fine," he assured her.

As he turned to face forward, his glance caught the pilot's profile beneath his helmet.

The man was missing the tip of his nose.

Fear instantly gripped Harrison's gut, even as he struggled to keep his features impassive. Could Rafiq have betrayed them?

Muwaffaq would either kill them in midair—two bodies in the midst of the desert would probably never be found. Or he'd fly them somewhere to question Julia. If the people he worked for thought she had information they wanted, they might try to torture it out of her.

He glanced back at her, his conscience burning with regret. In an effort to save Julia, he might have just signed her death warrant.

She squinted a look of confusion at the change in his expression, but he didn't dare try to signal anything. His only advantage was that Muwaffaq didn't know he was onto him. Besides, there was nothing to be gained by panicking Julia.

He sifted through his options.

If he tried to overpower the man, he could easily bring down the chopper. And Muwaffaq was probably armed.

If they landed, he'd have a better chance of overpowering him. But if they landed where Muwaffaq had planned, where reinforcements would certainly meet the chopper, he and Julia would have no chance at all.

He couldn't risk that.

Whatever he did had to happen in midair.

Adrenaline pumped through his system in time with the throbbing of the engine. He rested his hand in his lap, surreptitiously clicking open the metal buckle on his seat belt.

He painstakingly freed his arm, while making and discarding plans of attack.

But then Muwaffaq caught his movement, and his time was up.

Harrison gave a yell and elbowed Muwaffaq in the center of the throat.

The man's eyes bugged out, and he gasped a breath, his hands reflexively going for the injury.

"Harrison!" Julia cried out from the backseat as the chopper tilted and the engine whined.

Harrison flipped open the man's seat-belt buckle, then stretched to close his hands over the controls. He hadn't flown in at least a year, but all other options had meant certain death.

"Drag him back," he shouted to Julia, stuffing his feet on top of Muwaffaq's, scrambling to get some semblance of control over the tail rotor.

"What are you *doing?*" she demanded, even as she wiggled out of her own seat belt to follow his instructions.

Muwaffaq was gasping for breath. If he recovered from the blow, all hell would break loose.

As Julia clambered between the seats, she got a look at the man's nose.

She hesitated for a split second, and Muwaffaq took the opportunity and grabbed her by the throat.

Harrison was barely keeping them airborne. He didn't dare let go of the controls, but Julia was struggling and coughing.

He elbowed Muwaffaq again, this time catching him in the solar plexus.

The man's grip loosened enough that Julia pulled free and rocketed into the backseat.

"Shit," Harrison spat out, as Muwaffaq began to fight back.

He risked lifting a foot from the pedals and kicked at the man.

Muwaffaq grunted, and Harrison kicked again.

Then the helicopter door popped open.

Julia screamed.

Harrison gasped.

And Muwaffaq went tumbling into midair, his arms and legs flailing as he plummeted toward the dunes.

Harrison flopped into the pilot's seat, stabilized the aircraft, then slammed the door shut.

His breathing was labored, and his hands were shaking.

It took him a minute to get them flying straight.

When she finally spoke, Julia's voice was shaking, barely a rasp. "Is he dead?"

"Our altitude is five hundred feet."

"Then I guess he's dead."

Harrison didn't dare turn his attention to the backseat. "I'm more concerned about you. Are you all right?"

"I think so."

"Did he hurt your neck?"

"A little. I think it's bruised."

"Are there any sharp pains?"

"No."

Harrison breathed a sigh of relief. "I'll have you home soon."

"You know how to fly this thing?"

He couldn't help but chuckle at that. "If I didn't know how to fly this thing, we'd have hit the ground a long time ago."

She didn't answer, but he thought he heard the rustle of her nod.

"You sure you're all right?" he asked again. It was very likely she was in shock. If so, he wanted to keep her talking. And it was probably a good idea for him to keep himself talking, too.

"We just killed somebody," she said, horror and awe in her voice.

"No. Somebody tried to kill us. We defended ourselves."

"Is that a crime in the UAE?"

"You planning to confess to someone?"

She didn't answer.

"He was a *very* bad man, Julia. His body may never be found. And it's in our best interest that whoever he worked with not know we had anything to do with his death. Understand?"

Her voice was still shaking. "I guess."

He nodded to the other front seat. "Can you climb up here?"

"I'll try."

It took her a minute to maneuver her way between the two seats, but Harrison felt better once he could see her.

"Do up your seat belt."

She stared at him for a second, and then a weak laugh sputtered out of her.

"Safety first?" she asked in an incredulous voice, then she laughed harder.

Harrison couldn't help but grin in response. "You were great, by the way"

"Me?" she asked, pointing to her chest. "You were amazing. You can fly a helicopter. You beat up bad guys. And you married me and got me a great passport. I may have to be your slave for life."

"Deal," he said, without missing a beat.

She gestured toward him. "See that? You're funny, too."

"Who says I was joking?"

She hiccuped out a final laugh.

"Do up your seat belt," he told her again. The last thing he wanted was to have her whack her head because they hit some rough air.

"What about you?" she asked, but dutifully did up the buckle.

"Now you can do up mine."

She leaned over and fastened the clasp around his hips, her hand brushing his lap, practically making him leap out of the seat. He'd heard danger heightened a man's libido, and he guessed he now knew it was true.

By the time Harrison put the helicopter down on the grounds at Cadair, the sun had turned to an orange ball, sinking its way into the ocean. He flipped some switches and the motor went silent.

Julia tried to rally herself in the passenger seat. She was exhausted. She'd been through every emotion possible over the past two days, and she wanted nothing more than to crawl into bed and hide from the world.

But that was impossible. She still had to get out of the country, the sooner the better.

Before she could undo her seat belt, someone yanked open the passenger door, and she found herself looking into Nuri's strained face. She could swear the man looked pale.

"You are all right?" he asked, as if he actually cared. Then his attention jumped to Harrison and back again.

Harrison nodded. "We're okay."

"We found the real pilot. In a bathroom at the hangar." Nuri paused and glanced at Julia. "He was unconscious."

"I'm glad he isn't dead," said Harrison, releasing his own seat belt, then reaching over to undo Julia's.

She groaned as she moved forward in the seat. Her muscles were stiff, and her throat was still sore.

"You were not harmed?" asked Nuri, offering his hands to assist her. He didn't touch her, waiting for her to touch him instead.

When she placed her hands in his, his grasp was firm and sure. She stepped carefully down to the ground.

"There was a struggle," said Harrison, exiting the chopper and making his way around to Julia.

Nuri kept hold of her hands, and she realized he was staring at them. She glanced down and remembered the henna designs. She looked to Harrison, realizing that Nuri would understand what the designs symbolized.

Harrison took over from Nuri, his arm going firmly around her shoulders, and Nuri released her hands.

"Have the police been called?" Harrison asked.

Nuri shook his head. "We did not know what to tell them."

"Good. There's nothing to tell."

"And the man who took the helicopter?"

"We left him behind."

Nuri took one more glance at Julia's hand, then he nodded.

"Not a lot about this trip is worth discussing," said Harrison.

"I understand completely."

"Thank you."

"I'll take care of the helicopter."

"Take care of the man who was hurt, as well."

"Yes, sir," said Nuri.

Harrison turned to Julia and they started toward the palace. "Are you bribing that man to stay quiet?" she asked. A week ago she might have minded, but at the moment a bribe was perfectly okay by her.

"I'm taking care of his medical bills," said Harrison.

"Oh." She regretted that the question had made her sound suspicious.

Her legs grew more steady as they headed up the stone pathway that led to one of the side doors of the palace.

"And anything else his family needs," Harrison continued.

They walked a little farther in silence.

"So, yeah," said Harrison. "I guess you could say I'm bribing him to keep him quiet."

Harrison was using the special privileges of the rich. He was bribing people to keep her safe. In a bizarre way, it warmed her heart.

"Thank you," she told him. "One more time."

Harrison gave her a squeeze. "That's what husbands do. Let's go up the back way. And you can get some sleep."

"What about getting out of the country?"

"We'll take care of that tomorrow. Do you want the same room?"

She hesitated, not ready to leave Harrison just yet. He'd come to represent strength and security in a world that was completely off-kilter. She was also still worried about the police. And she was more than a little rattled by the altercation in the helicopter.

"This is going to sound pathetic," she told him, pausing at the bottom of the veranda stairs.

He waited.

"I don't want to be alone."

He gave her a teasing smile and smoothed her hair from her face. "Are you feeling sentimental about your wedding night?"

She rolled her eyes. "I'm feeling afraid of the local thugs and the police."

But deep down inside, she was feeling sentimental about her wedding night. Because, no matter what the language, she'd married Harrison today. It was his name on her passport, and they were bound in the eyes of the law.

She glanced down. She might not have a ring on her finger, but she did have the stamp of their wedding all over her hands.

"It will wash off in a couple of weeks," he told her.

"Fitting," she mused. "Most women get a diamond that lasts forever."

"You want a diamond?"

She glanced up. "That would be silly."

And it would make more of this than there was. As

soon as she was out of the country, either she or Harrison would start divorce proceedings. Six months from now, this would be nothing but a strange footnote in her life.

He gazed at her with a smirk and a challenging lift of his eyebrows. "So which will it be? In the name of protection, do you want me in your bed, or just in your room?"

Good question.

"Lord *Rochester,*" Leila's voice sang as she appeared at the veranda rail. She pushed herself off and trotted down the stairs to greet them. "You are back."

"We are back."

"So all is well?" she asked, her expression worried.

"Yes. It is now."

She smiled. "Are you hungry?"

"We're tired," said Harrison.

Leila reached for Julia's hands.

And before Julia could hide them, Leila spotted the henna.

Her eyes went wide, and she stared at Harrison. "Brittany?"

"It's complicated," said Harrison.

Julia jumped in. "This keeping it a secret isn't working out so well."

Leila rapidly shook her head. "I will not tell a soul."

"It's temporary," Julia explained. "Just until I get out of the country."

Leila nodded, but her eyes were still wide.

"We can rely on your discretion?" Harrison asked in a stern voice, clearly driving home the point.

Leila bobbed her head.

He smiled at her. "Good. Can you help Julia with a bath?"

"Of course."

Julia resisted an urge to reach for Harrison. Leila was fine company. She genuinely liked the girl. But she doubted Leila could fight off kidnappers or assassins should any of them sneak into the palace.

"I'll come up later," he said to Julia. "We can talk then."

About whether or not to sleep together.

She supposed she should come up with her own answer to that question.

In her wildest dreams, Brittany never thought making love would last twelve hours.

She and Alex had barely left the bed all day long. They'd ordered room service a couple of times, and took a bath at one point, and now they were snuggled under the comforter. He was stroking her hair and telling her a story that was supposed to be about his first parachute jump. But, so far, they hadn't made it past his tenth birthday.

"The race was the talk of the school," said Alex.

His cell phone rang.

"Don't you move," he told her, kissing the tip of her nose.

She smiled in response. "Are you kidding? Before I find out how it ends?"

The phone rang again while he gazed at her with a goofy smile. Then he slipped from beneath the covers and tracked down his suit jacket, retrieving the chiming phone, his back toward her.

"Yeah?"

She stared unashamedly at the play of muscles across his shoulders, his taut buttocks and muscular legs.

"You're back?" he said into the phone, lifting one of the hotel bathrobes and slipping into it.

"We're in Abu Dhabi," Alex said into the phone. "The Emirates Palace."

Brittany sat up, pinning the comforter across her chest with her arms, trying to figure out who Alex would reveal that information to.

He turned to face her, and she raised a quizzical eyebrow.

"Julia okay?" asked Alex, with a meaningful look at Brittany.

Harrison.

Alex was talking to Harrison.

A weight settled in the pit of Brittany's stomach. Her soon-to-be fiancé had been fleeing through the desert on a rescue mission while she had been frolicking in bed with his employee.

Alex saw her expression and shook his head.

Ignoring him, she scrambled from the bed and stuffed her arms into the other robe. She scooped up her clothes and headed for the bathroom. But Alex grasped her arm on the way by and refused to let her go.

"We'll be back tomorrow," he said to Harrison.

She glared at him, trying to wrestle her arm free. But private-school phys-ed class was no match for navy basic training, and she didn't gain an inch.

"You are?" he asked Harrison.

He finally let go of her arm, but it was only to wrap his own firmly around her waist and jerk her against him. She didn't dare yell, didn't dare utter a word, but that didn't stop her from kicking her heel into his shin.

"I'll talk to you then," said Alex.

Brittany twisted her head to glare at him.

"Glad to hear it," said Alex.

Then he flipped the phone shut.

She wrenched against him. "I don't believe you did that!"

His arm remained firmly around her waist, holding her back against his chest. "Where were you going?"

"To get dressed."

His tone was implacable. "You agreed to stay put."

"That's before you started talking to Harrison."

"So what?"

"I'm supposed to lie there naked in your bed with my fiancé on the phone?"

"He's not your fiancé."

"We have an understanding." Well, they sort of had an understanding. She presumed they had an understanding.

If there wasn't an understanding, why had Harrison invited her to Dubai in the first place?

"We agreed you were free," said Alex.

"We hung our consciences on a technicality."

"Yes, we did. And we can't put your virginity back, and I'm still quitting my job in the morning. The only thing we have to decide, Brittany, is whether we spend one last night together or alone."

"Alone," she asserted.

He was silent.

Then his warm lips touched the crook of her neck.

"You sure?" he whispered, all trace of frustration gone from his tone. His hand splayed against her stomach.

"Yes." She nodded.

He nibbled his way up her neck, drawing her earlobe into his mouth.

Despite herself, she felt her body respond to his gentle touch.

"Really sure?" he rumbled in her ear.

"Really sure," she responded, but it came out on a sigh.

He smoothed her hair back from her temple and placed a kiss there. "Because it won't change a thing."

"I know," she agreed. They couldn't undo the day. And she couldn't undo her feelings. Alex had been a magical lover—funny, patient and gentle. She never would have imagined it of him.

But the day was over. She had a life to go back to, and that life included her family, traditions, responsibilities and Harrison.

"I'm not asking you to make love again," Alex told her, releasing her and gently turning her to face him. He placed his hands on her shoulders, and there was something vulnerably earnest in his expression. "I only want you to sleep in my arms."

Emotion tightened her chest, and she fought it with all her might.

"He gets you forever," Alex whispered. "Give me this one night."

Brittany's heart all but melted.

She gave in and nodded.

Then she nodded harder, wanting it every bit as much as he did.

He scooped her into his arms and crossed to the bed.

He laid her down, then climbed in beside her, sliding her, spoon style, against the warmth of his body.

They lay there quietly for a few minutes. She forced herself to stay in the moment. There was no yesterday, no tomorrow, just now and Alex, the hum of the ceiling fan and the softness of the bed that cocooned them in a fantasy.

"Finish your story?" she asked him.

"The lawn mower," he said, picking up where he'd

left off. "In my dad's garage. If we wanted to win the go-kart race, my older brother, Jacob, and I needed four wheels and an internal combustion engine."

"You turned your father's lawn mower into a go-kart?"

"Not exactly."

Brittany breathed a little sigh of relief. The worst she'd done as a child was steal the foil-and-chocolate decorations from the Christmas tree.

"We built a wood and scrap-metal frame, bolted on the wheels and connected a belt drive to the lawn mower engine. I thought it was fine, but Jacob insisted we needed more torque if we were going to beat those Brubaker boys."

"What's torque?"

"Power. So we disassembled the rototiller. Man, that did the trick. That puppy was fast."

"Weren't you scared of your parents?"

He rested his chin against the top of her head. "We had it all planned. Dad mowed the lawns on Sunday. We'd race Saturday morning, reassemble everything that afternoon, and nobody'd be any the wiser."

"Did it work?"

Alex chuckled. "Does it sound to you like it would work?"

"How would I know? Forget about torque, I've never seen a rototiller."

"It didn't work," said Alex.

Even though it was years in the past, Brittany felt her stomach tense with nervous anticipation.

"The good news is, we won the trophy. Got that baby up to fifteen miles an hour."

She couldn't help but grin at the pride that was evident in his voice all these years later. "And the bad news?"

"By ten o'clock on Saturday night, we realized we'd misplaced a few of the lawn mower and rototiller parts. My mom realized we weren't in bed. And my dad realized he needed to teach us a lesson."

Brittany cringed. "Ouch."

"Ouch is right. But it was still worth it. We were boys. We accepted spankings as the cost of having fun. Besides, the go-kart was nothing compared to our next project."

"I'm afraid to ask."

"We decided to try parachuting off the roof."

"Did your parents by any chance *insist* that you join the navy?"

"They thought it would improve my moral fiber."

"And did it?"

"Not really, but it was a whole lot of fun."

"Fun?" Brittany had seen enough movies to know the military wasn't fun.

"Basic training was a piece of cake. There wasn't anything a drill sergeant could do or say that my dad and older brother hadn't been doing my entire life. And, after we got through basic, they let us blow things up, run obstacle courses and learn to use high-tech equipment. I thought I'd died and gone to adventure camp."

Brittany found herself smiling. "I am so glad I'm not having your children."

He went silent, and she immediately cringed.

Then she flipped onto her back to look up at him. "That was thoughtless. I'm sorry."

He brushed a lock of hair from her face, his expression teasing rather than hurt. "I have a feeling you'd balance me out, Miss Pure-As-The-Driven-Snow."

"Not anymore," she reminded him, the memory suddenly blooming in her brain.

"No," he agreed, his smile disappearing. "Not anymore."

She was overcome with the desire to kiss him.

He obviously saw it in her eyes, because he leaned down, and his lips softly met her own, sweet, tender, so full of life and excitement.

Just here and now, she told herself. That was all they'd ever have.

Chapter Fourteen

"This is our last night together," said Harrison as he pushed the bedroom door shut.

An hour had gone by since they'd separated, and Julia's heart gave a little hitch at the sight of him.

"It's also our wedding night," he continued, starting across the floor to where she was curled up in an armchair.

He came to a halt directly in front of her. "What do you suppose the odds are I'm staying out of your bed?"

Julia had finished reporting in to Melanie, so she set the cordless phone down on the end table.

"Slim?" she offered, as his gaze swept the simple gauzy, white dress she'd slipped on after her bath.

"Nil," he responded, his attention returning to her face.

"Nil," she agreed with a nod.

They might as well make the inevitable decision up front. Real life might start again tomorrow, but tonight was theirs if they wanted it.

He reached for her hands and drew them up to the light, turning them over to inspect the palms. "If they did this right, my initials are somewhere in here. Tradition says that I'm not allowed to make love with you until I find them in the pattern."

"What if Rania and her mother did it wrong?"

His twinkling gaze met hers. "Then it's going to be a very, very long night."

She wiggled her feet out to where he could see them. "There's more down there."

"Not a problem. I'm a patient man."

She couldn't resist. "That really hasn't been my experience so far."

"Are you tossing out a dare?" he asked, with a teasing touch of incredulity.

She gave a little shrug. "Why not?"

His smile broadened, and he turned her hands to inspect the backs.

"Is it like a bridal shower?" she asked, remembering the surreal experience. "Rania and Habeeba talked at me the entire time. They had to know I didn't understand a word."

Harrison's expression turned grim. "That's really unfortunate."

Julia became worried. "That they talked?"

"That you didn't understand it. Arabs are very sensual people, Julia. Rania and Habeeba were imparting the wisdom of the ages. All the secret, erotic arts are passed down from generation to generation at the henna ceremony."

Julia opened her mouth in mock dismay. "And I *missed* it?"

"Worse than that. *I'm* missing it." He gave a long-suffering sigh. "Why couldn't you have learned Arabic instead of French?"

She withdrew her hands and folded her arms over her chest. "Excuse me? Are you suggesting my erotic arts could stand improvement?"

"There's nothing wrong with a little variety," he deadpanned.

"Are you *trying* to ruin the evening?"

"I'd be happy to give you a few pointers. The groom gets an earful at an Arab wedding, too, you know."

Really? Julia shimmied to her feet and gave him a saucy grin, pointing to her chest and putting a lilt in her voice. "On how to please *me?*"

He chuckled low. "You are one lucky woman."

"I think I'll be the judge of that. She slid her palms up his chest, tipping her head and coming up on her toes for his kiss. "Go ahead, give me your best shot."

"You sound like you're planning to grade me in the morning."

"You bet I am."

"Okay," he agreed. But instead of kissing her, as she'd expected, he tapped his index finger against her nose. "You wait here."

"Where are you going?"

"To get the ropes and feathers."

She felt her eyes go wide.

"Oh, baby," he drawled.

He was joking.

He had to be joking.

But an unexpected excitement mixed with the trepidation in her belly.

She coughed out a laugh to cover it. "I have to wonder what the hell those people are *doing* out in the desert."

"They're definitely not smiling because of the dust and the camels."

"You are *not* tying me up." She truly didn't think she'd like that.

"Don't be a spoilsport."

"Given my recent near-kidnapping experience, I have bondage issues."

He pretended to contemplate the problem. "What about the feathers?"

She thought about that. Feathers didn't sound awful. In fact, they sounded kind of...interesting.

"The blindfold?" he pressed.

"Maybe we should stick to you finding your initials."

"We can start there," he agreed, drawing her back into his arms. "Then we'll negotiate the rest."

He leaned down and kissed her mouth.

She reflexively parted her lips, tipping her head, fitting perfectly to the heat and suction of his mouth. Memories swamped her senses, and she felt as though she belonged in his arms.

He flipped open a button on her dress, then another, and another.

"One of the rules of henna," he whispered between sensual kisses, "is that you have to be naked while I find my initials."

"Now you're just making things up."

"I swear it's true."

In the end, it didn't matter. Because Julia wanted to get

naked for Harrison, and she wanted Harrison to get naked, too. She wanted to press her skin against his and hold on tight for as long as she could possibly get away with it.

He pushed the dress from her shoulders, and it slunk to the floor. Her bra and underwear were simple, white against her tanned skin. He gazed down along the line of her body.

"You're so beautiful," he breathed.

She'd always thought of herself as ordinary, but she liked the desire she saw reflected in his steel eyes.

Her fingers went to the buttons on his shirt. He was back in Western dress—a crisp, white shirt and a pair of gray slacks. She pushed the smooth button through the hole, remembering the play of muscles on his broad chest, even as she revealed them one more time.

When she got to the bottom, she tugged the shirttails from his waistband, separating the fabric and running her fingers over his warm, taut skin. She leaned forward to kiss his pecs, leaving a damp, shining circle.

He cupped her chin and tipped it up, his lips hot and mobile where they came down on her mouth. She fought the distraction, dislodging the button of his slacks.

One of his hands went to her back, unfastening her bra, the fabric slipping away even as his hand slid down below the waistband of her panties to knead her soft bottom.

Then he slipped off the panties and stepped out of his slacks. He lifted her into his arms and carried her to the big bed, depositing her on a billowy, satin comforter.

He dropped to his knees, his strong hands sliding over her body, across her belly, over her thighs to her knees and her feet. He repositioned himself, gazing at the pattern on her left foot.

"H.W.A.B.R.W." he muttered.

She curled up on her elbow. "I don't think my foot's that big."

He ran his fingertip along the arch. "It doesn't really matter. I can't read Arabic. Ahmed translates for me."

"Now *there's* a flaw in the game plan."

His finger stopped on the tip of her ankle. "This might be a letter." He cocked his head. "Or maybe a flower." He kissed the ankle. "A lily? A poppy? Or maybe a scroll?"

Julia smiled down at the top of his dark head, feeling calm for the first time in days. "I'm thinking this is going to take a while."

In response, he promptly kissed her calf, then the curve of her knee, her thigh, her hip, then the crest of her breast.

Sparks sizzled through her body, and she gasped in a breath. "Wow."

He pulled back. "Is this too fast?"

"You got something in between?"

He slipped onto the bed next to her and gathered her in his arms. "I can see this is going to be quite the challenge."

"I'm a fickle woman."

"Fickle is fine. There's nothing worse than predictability."

She slipped a thigh across his hip, holding him closer still. "I have tried very, very hard to keep your life exciting."

"And I appreciate the effort."

She smiled into his eyes. But suddenly she was overcome with the enormity of leaving him tomorrow.

They both slowly sobered, their breathing synchronized. The overhead fan whirred off the seconds, and his thumb drew circles on her palm.

"Do you feel married?" she asked him.

It took him a minute to respond. "A little bit."

She nodded. "Me, too." Then she paused. "It's funny. I didn't expect it. There was no dress, no ring, and they could have been reciting the Declaration of Independence for all I could tell."

"They weren't," he said, his voice low with conviction.

Then he unexpectedly rose from the bed.

She was suddenly cold, almost frightened. "Harrison?"

But he came back quickly, something shiny in his hand.

She blinked it into focus and realized it was a diamond ring.

Her stomach contracted in a rush of emotion.

"It's an heirloom, but we'll need it tomorrow," he said, reaching for her hand.

She watched him slide it over the knuckle of her ring finger, where the large, empress diamond sparkled against the henna pattern.

"I wish you hadn't done that," she said, feeling almost weepy.

"I don't want any glitches going through Immigration," he responded. "A bride without a ring may raise questions."

She nodded.

That was very logical of him, and she was being silly in letting it get to her. This was still a marriage of convenience, and a very temporary one at that. Harrison belonged to Brittany, not to Julia.

"Is there something wrong?" he asked, peering into her eyes.

She shook her head and forced a smile.

He stretched back out on the bed, wrapped his arms

around her, and pulled her into the cradle of his body. She all but melted into his strength as his kisses found the crook of her neck.

She turned to face him, offering up her mouth. They melded together as their lovemaking took on a sense of urgency.

Deep in sleep, Julia whimpered in Harrison's arms.

She twitched against him and thrashed her head to one side of the pillow.

"Shh," he whispered in her ear, smoothing her hair, trying to soothe away her nightmare. "You're dreaming."

She whimpered louder.

"Julia," he tried. "Wake up, sweetheart."

Her foot kicked and she struggled to cry out.

He spoke louder. "Julia."

She stilled. Her eyes blinked open in the dim light.

"You were having a dream," he repeated.

In response, she turned and clung to him, burying her face in his shoulder, muffling her voice.

"Hey," he said softly.

"We were in the helicopter again," she hiccuped. "You were falling. And Muwaffaq was laughing and laughing."

She drew a shuddering breath, and Harrison realized she was more rattled by the experience than he'd thought.

"Everything was in slow motion," she continued. "I reached for you. I could see the patterns on my hands. They were codes. And I knew, I just *knew,* if I could only read Arabic, I could save you. But I couldn't read Arabic, and you were falling…"

Harrison hugged her tight, his heart aching, her body feeling fragile in his arms. She'd been through so much, and she obviously hadn't had enough time to recover. And he still felt the need to protect her. It wasn't some kind of an on-off switch.

How could he send her away all alone?

"You're safe," he reassured her. "Nothing can happen here. I have security all over the stable."

She nodded, but she was still shaking.

"And I'll take you home," he said, making up his mind.

He'd planned to buy her a first-class ticket to Lexington. But he'd take his own plane instead.

She drew a breath. "You sure the passport thing will work?"

"It will work," he said, drawing back to reassure her with his eyes. "Besides, I'm coming with you to make sure."

"You mean to the airport?"

He rested his head on his own pillow so they were eye to eye. "To Lexington."

She didn't say anything, simply blinked at him quizzically.

"I want to talk to the Prestons," he lied.

While he did want to talk to the Prestons, there was no need to do it in person. His telephones were working just fine.

Truth was, he simply wanted to stay with Julia. He had no intention of examining the reasons why. He was just going with his instincts.

He'd get her safely back to Lexington, then he'd come back to Dubai and find out who the hell had attacked them in the desert, and why the police were interested in her. The subject wasn't closed, not by a long shot. But he was getting her out of harm's way before he stirred up anything else.

After a pause, she said, "I'm really glad you're alive."

He smiled at her. "So am I."

"Who do you think they are?"

"Nobody who can get to you now."

"I've been thinking about it," she said. "Why are they scared of me?"

An excellent question. One Harrison had been pondering himself. "Maybe Muwaffaq poisoned Millions to Spare, and he knew you could identify him."

"But why did he poison Millions to Spare? And how did he get the police to help him?"

"The same way I got the police to help me. Money."

"He bribed them?"

Harrison didn't believe for a second that Muwaffaq had the power or wherewithal to bribe the entire police force. "It could be that simple," he told Julia.

"I'm glad he's gone," she said. "I'd rather he was in prison," she hastily added. "But I'm glad he's gone."

"I'm glad he's gone, too," said Harrison. And he didn't particularly care that the man was dead. Muwaffaq had likely murdered his horse. And it had been him or them, simple as that. Harrison would do it again if Julia was in danger.

"Nothing like this ever happens in Kentucky."

He smoothed her hair back from her face, giving himself an excuse to touch her.

"Tell me about Kentucky," he said, hoping to turn her mind to happier topics.

"It's green," she responded, relaxing into her pillow. "And it smells fresh all year long. There's a creek off my deck, with trails along both banks. If I didn't travel so much, I'd get a dog. He'd love the outdoors, and we'd walk for miles and miles."

"What kind of a dog?"

"A Dalmatian. Or maybe a Labrador. Something with lots of stamina. I'd throw sticks in the water and Herman would retrieve them."

"Herman?"

"It was my grandfather's name."

"Oh, in that case, great name."

"What about you? Do you like dogs?"

"We have two golden retrievers at the house in Windsor."

"Windsor?"

"It's a borough just outside London. We have a lovely, little country estate there. It's perfect for dogs and horses."

"What are their names?"

"Alpha and Epsilon."

"You don't think that's a little pretentious?"

"Maybe compared to Herman."

She nudged him with her elbow. "Don't you be messing with Herman. He'll be sleeping with me long after you're gone."

"Maybe, but I suspect I'm a better kisser."

She made a show of considering that statement. "I'll have to get back to you on that."

"So, aside from kissing dogs—" he kept the conversation going "—what else do you do in Lexington?"

"Tennis."

"Really?"

She nodded. "There are courts in the park down the street, and a group of us in the condo development that like to play."

"We've got some nice courts in Windsor."

"On the little estate?"

Was it his imagination, or was there a thread of disdain in that question?

"Yes, on the estate. Do you have something against private tennis courts?"

"They take up a lot of space."

"We have a lot of space."

"I don't. But I'm thinking of putting in a gazebo some day."

"We have a nice gazebo." He couldn't stop himself from hoping she'd decide to come for a visit.

"Is there anything you don't have in Windsor?"

He could think of one thing. Her. But he wasn't about to say that out loud. "We don't have an orchard."

She sighed expansively. "How *do* you manage?"

"Quit being such a reverse snob. It's a nice estate."

"Apparently it needs an orchard."

"Cherry trees," said Harrison decisively. "Acres of little white blossoms followed by plump, purple, Bing cherries."

"You could hang a swing from one of the trees."

"That would be nice."

"And your perfect daughter, in her little white dress and patent leather shoes, could swing back and forth while she watched you play tennis."

"I'd beat you," he said, putting Julia into the fantasy. "I've had lessons, and I have a longer reach."

"You think I'm coming all the way to Windsor to play tennis?"

Harrison immediately realized what he'd done.

"Or I could come to Lexington," he offered, to cover up the blunder.

"How often do you play?"

"Once or twice a month."

"Ha! You're on." There was satisfaction in her voice.
"I play three times a week."

"Really? I'm up for a match. Care to make it a little
interesting?"

She leaned up on her elbow. "What did you have in
mind?"

He matched her posture. "You win, I build you a
gazebo. I win, you name your dog Harrison."

"You'd build me a gazebo? As in, cutting boards and
hammering nails?"

"More along the lines of write a check to a carpen-
ter," he said honestly. "But, yes, I'd build you a gazebo."

She smiled, and he realized in that moment that he'd
do pretty much anything to make her happy. The re-
alization was both exhilarating and frightening.

Julia struggled against cold, hard terror as they
crossed the airport terminal, heading for the security
check-in. She was about to present herself to the very
people who'd been hunting her down. And all she had
for protection was a little red book, along with Harrison's assurance that the men with the guns would
respect it.

"This way," said Harrison, pointing to a short lineup off
to one side of the security area designated for diplomats.

She felt like an imposter.

"Relax," he murmured.

She nodded, but she could feel the sweat gathering
on her palms.

They walked quickly up to the wicket, and Harrison
handed the uniformed man both passports.

The guard swiped Harrison's through a machine and
pressed a button on his keyboard. He stared at the screen

for a moment, pressed another button, stamped the passport and handed it back.

Then he swiped Julia's.

His eyes narrowed, and he looked up at her.

He said something to Harrison in Arabic.

Harrison answered and produced their marriage certificate.

The man read the document. He typed something into his keyboard, and she could see the exact second he found her old identity.

He must have pressed some kind of secret alarm, because three more security guards descended on the little kiosk.

Harrison snagged her hand and squeezed. "Don't worry," he muttered.

She was past worrying. She'd gone straight to petrified. This was it. They were going to arrest her here and now.

The guards seemed to be arguing amongst themselves.

One of the new guards picked up a phone.

She wanted to ask Harrison what they were saying. But she was too afraid of the answer. All she could do was stand mute and watch four stern-looking Arabs decide her fate.

The guard set down the phone.

He shot a rapid-fire question at Julia.

Harrison answered.

He asked another.

Harrison's expression and stance didn't waver. He provided another answer.

That guard looked at Julia's passport.

He read the marriage certificate.

Finally, scowling, he banged the stamp down on her passport and handed everything back to Harrison.

Harrison put an arm firmly around her shoulders and ushered her past the kiosk.

She didn't say a word as they rounded the corner and moved out of sight.

"You're through," said Harrison with a squeeze.

Her legs were shaking, and she didn't think she was capable of forming an actual word.

They turned down a narrow hallway and came to a podium with another guard.

"What's this?" she asked hoarsely.

"Relax. We're done. This is only to get into the private boarding gates. We're taking my jet."

"You have a jet?"

"I have a jet." He gave his passport to the guard.

The man checked a list, smiled at Harrison, and let them through.

Julia couldn't help looking back over her shoulder.

But nobody was coming after her.

She was out of the UAE.

She was going home.

Chapter Fifteen

Julia had always been intimidated by the Prestons'
sprawling brick house. But having experienced the
palace at Cadair, she now realized Melanie's mother,
Jenna, had made the large house homey, even intimate
with her old-world decorating touches. Where Cadair
was cavernous as a museum, the Preston house was
filled with cushions, pottery and horse pictures.

As they often did, some of the family members had
gathered in the large room behind the west veranda. The
outside lights showed a windswept, leaf-strewn deck
with light rain falling. But inside it was warm, and the
wide-screen television broadcasted a Formula Gold
night race out of California.

Julia knew that Melanie's grandfather, Hugh Preston,
was a friend and fan of racer Demetri Lucas, so the
family tried to watch Formula Gold as often as possible.

"Mom, Dad, Grandpa?" sang Melanie. "Look who's home?"

Jenna glanced up from where she was chopping vegetables, while Thomas, Jenna's husband, and Hugh looked up from the race.

Jenna's smile beamed as she dried her hands on a towel and came around the breakfast bar. "So wonderful to have you home, Julia."

She gave Julia a quick hug.

"And this is Harrison Rochester," Melanie continued with the introductions.

Both men came to their feet to shake hands with Harrison and welcome Julia back.

At the same time, Robbie appeared and joined the conversation.

Jenna muted the race, while Thomas offered Kentucky sipping whiskey all around.

There was plenty of comfortable seating, and Julia ended up on a love seat next to Harrison.

"What's on your hands?" asked Melanie as Thomas handed Julia a drink.

Julia momentarily froze.

"A Middle Eastern tradition," Harrison put in smoothly. "While we were at Khandi Oasis, some of the women wanted to decorate Julia's hands."

"It's henna," Julia put in. "It'll wear off in a couple of weeks."

"It's pretty," Jenna offered.

"Thank you," said Julia. "I like it, too."

She caught Harrison's gaze and had to struggle to keep her features even.

"Can you explain what happened to your horse?" asked Hugh in his usual booming voice.

Harrison set down his drink on the table beside him. "Not yet," he admitted. "I'll be back in Dubai in a few days, and I plan to launch an extensive investigation. But I wanted to get Julia out of the country first."

"Any problems getting out?" asked Melanie.

"We were worried sick," said Jenna from where she sat next to Thomas on a longer couch. "Imagine, people chasing you like that."

They'd had to share the fact that both the police and criminals were after Julia, since it could impact on Leopold's Legacy's investigation.

"It went surprisingly smoothly," said Harrison. "Any news here on Leopold's Legacy?"

"We're struggling with the registry records," said Robbie. "A pivotal employee, Ross Ingliss, has suddenly quit, and that's caused increased technical complications."

"I assume you'll check on other Apollo's Ice foals?" asked Harrison.

"Just as soon as humanly possible," put in Thomas.

"There's the checkered flag," called Hugh, raising his glass to the screen. "Not a win, but he's in the top five again."

Melanie's oldest brother, Andrew, joined them. "Bad news," he said, taking in the crowd of people, then he noticed Harrison.

Harrison came to his feet and held out his hand to Andrew. "Harrison Rochester."

"Andrew Preston," Andrew returned with a shake. "Probably a good thing you're here."

"What happened?" asked Hugh.

Andrew eased himself into one of the remaining seats. "We've been banned from racing by the International Thoroughbred Racing Federation."

"In *all* countries?" asked Melanie.

"How can they do that?" Robbie demanded.

Julia's heart sank. She knew Melanie and Robbie were counting on international races for Something to Talk About. They were planning a trip to their cousin's stable in Australia to give the horse an opportunity to race.

Andrew looked to Harrison. "The negative publicity surrounding Leopold's Legacy now stretches as far as Dubai."

"They know about Millions to Spare?" asked Thomas.

"I had to disclose it," said Andrew.

Hugh nodded his concurrence. "We have done *nothing* wrong," he declared. "We will be exonerated."

"But how long will it take?" asked Melanie.

"It will take as long as it takes," said Jenna, her voice calm and steady. She looked to her husband. "We'll make it through somehow."

Thomas squeezed her hand, and a look passed between them—one that said they were two people who had weathered storms before and understood each other in a way no one else ever could.

Julia couldn't help glancing at Harrison. They'd weathered their own storms. And there were things about their time together in Dubai that the world would never discover.

Harrison finished his drink and stood. "I should head back into the city," he announced, causing Julia's stomach to contract.

Was this it? Was it all over?

"How can you say that?" asked Jenna, rising from her seat. "Dinner will be ready in half an hour."

"I don't want to impose," said Harrison.

Julia couldn't take her gaze off him. Was he getting back on his plane tonight? She hadn't thought about that. She'd promised Melanie she would stay a day or two, but she'd assumed she'd have a chance to say goodbye to Harrison in private.

If he walked out now, all she'd get was a handshake and a polite nod along with everyone else.

"It's no imposition at all," Jenna insisted.

"I thought I should find a hotel room before it got too late," he continued.

"Nonsense," said Jenna with a dismissive wave of her hand. "You can stay in one of the guest cabins."

"Julia's in the magnolia cabin," said Melanie. "But there are others to choose from. They're very comfortable."

Harrison glanced around at the expressions of the other family members. "If you're sure," he said.

"Of course we're sure," said Hugh. "Don't know what it's like over there in the Middle East, but around here we're hospitable."

"And I thank you for that," Harrison said to Hugh, while Julia experienced a wave of relief.

"Can I get some help setting the table?" asked Jenna. "It's our cook and housekeeper's night off."

Andrew and Melanie both got to their feet.

Julia stood, as well, but Jenna waved her back down. "You're company tonight," said Jenna.

"I wasn't company last time I was here."

"You're tired from changing time zones," said Melanie.

That much was true. Julia was definitely feeling tired and disoriented. Maybe that's why the thought of Harrison leaving had been so painful.

* * *

After the Preston house and the surrounding staff cabins went dark and quiet, Harrison crossed the lawn and rapped on Julia's door.

Soft light shone through the front curtains, and he heard footsteps patter on the floor inside. She opened the door, dressed in a navy T-shirt, a pair of casual, gray sweatpants and bare feet. Her hair was loose and her face was scrubbed free of makeup. But her blue eyes shone bright and beautiful, and he knew he was in way over his head.

"You should tell me to go away."

"Go away," she murmured.

"You don't mean that."

She didn't answer. Instead she gave him a resigned smile and stepped out of the way, allowing him entrance to the small, cozy living room.

Her cabin was a mirror image of his next door. It had a combination living room and kitchen across the front, with two small bedrooms and a bathroom in the back. The larger bedroom was furnished with a double bed, colorful comforter and plump pillows, while the smaller one had steel bunks with rolled-up sleeping bags at the foot.

"I promised myself I wouldn't do this," Harrison told her honestly.

She was home. She was safe. And there was no more reason for him to hang around.

But his resolve had faltered. He simply couldn't lie in bed fifty feet from her and not find his way to her side.

"Promised not to do what?" she asked.

He took in an opened horse magazine on the plaid couch and a steaming mug on the end table. It smelled like hot chocolate, and he suddenly wanted nothing more than to hole up here with her for as long as she'd let him.

"Harrison?" she prompted, and he realized she was waiting for his answer.

"Pretend this is real," he admitted, moving closer to her. "Pretend we can be together, and the world outside the two of us doesn't exist."

She tipped her head, keeping eye contact as he grew closer. "I'm afraid it does."

He reached out and took her hands. "That's why I told myself to stay away. That's why I'm leaving tomorrow, putting an ocean between us."

"You have to go back to Brittany."

"I know I do," he acknowledged. "Being my wife is a terrible job. But Brittany knows what she's getting into. She can help me. She can support our kids."

Harrison realized the person he was trying to convince was himself. Because, over the past few hours, he'd been starting to think the unthinkable. Keeping Julia.

She tugged her hands away, a trace of hurt in her voice as she turned away. "Unlike me?"

"Is that what you want?" he dared ask.

"I only wanted to get out of Dubai." Her tone was stronger now. "The last time I checked, that's the only thing I signed up for."

Her words hit him like a sledgehammer. Somehow, he'd built it up in his mind as being something more, much more.

"Of course," he answered her back.

How conceited did he have to be to assume Julia would want him in her life? His money and title meant nothing to her. She was grateful for his help. That was it.

"I guess this is goodbye," he told her.

She nodded without turning around.

"I'll be on the jet early tomorrow."

"I understand."

"I'll send you…" He couldn't bring himself to say divorce papers. "I'll send you whatever we need," he told her instead. "I'll take care of it."

Her voice was small. "Thank you."

He wished she'd turn around. He wanted to see her face one more time. Hell, he wanted to see all of her one more time, and hold her in his arms, and inhale the soft scent of her hair, hear the laughter in her voice. But that was impossible.

"Goodbye," she whispered.

"Goodbye," he echoed, reaching for the door handle.

When Julia woke up the next morning, her heart ached, and her throat was sore from choking back tears.

Somebody was knocking on the cabin door. So she rolled out of the warm four-poster and slipped her feet into a pair of knit slippers. Still dressed in the T-shirt and sweatpants she'd borrowed from Melanie last night, she padded across the hardwood floor.

She didn't know whether or not to hope it was Harrison. She thought she'd done a credible job last night, refraining from cracking in front of him, even though he'd broken her heart and then stomped it to dust. Better to leave things that way.

Still, the thought of seeing him again…

But it was Melanie. Dressed in jeans, boots and a red wool jacket, she carried two travel mugs and a basket of muffins.

"Breakfast?" she asked.

Julia nodded and tried to force the kinks out of her sore body. "What time is it?"

"Nearly noon."

Julia couldn't believe she'd slept that long.

Her glance found its way past Melanie to the cabin where Harrison had slept last night. She wished she'd had it in her to give him a final thank-you and a proper goodbye, but she'd been teetering close to the edge of her emotional control. She'd fallen hard for him, and it was going to take some time for her to heal.

Melanie strolled into the cabin, and Julia locked out the chill. She cranked up the heater then joined Melanie in the living room. After taking her coffee and one of the blueberry muffins, she settled into an armchair and draped a knitted throw across her lap.

"It was ninety-five in Dubai," she reminded Melanie.

Melanie curled up in the corner of the couch with her own mug of coffee. "So, go ahead, give me the details."

Julia wasn't sure she could share much more. She couldn't tell anyone the details of Muwaffaq's death, or her marriage. Which meant she couldn't let anyone see she was upset.

"Not much more to tell," said Julia, struggling to keep her emotions at bay.

"Ha!" countered Melanie. "Let's start with what's up between you and Harrison."

Julia tensed. Anything but that. "What do you mean?"

"I saw the way he looked at you."

"We've been through a lot together. What with the police, and the bad guys."

"It's more than just that." Melanie waggled her eyebrows. "He obviously has the hots for you."

Julia steeled herself for her next words, hating that she couldn't tell Melanie the truth, but needing to shut this conversation down. "He's gone home to propose to another woman."

Melanie's eyes narrowed. "That doesn't make sense."

"Sure, it does. They're childhood friends, from the same social class—"

"You're not going to get all 'you rich are different' on me again, are you?"

"I confess," said Julia honestly, "I've come to better appreciate the value of wealth over the past week."

"Good," said Melanie, taking a sip of her coffee. "That's something then. Learn anything else while you were away?"

"That the desert is really, really hot, and it is amazingly easy to bribe the police."

"Hence, your new appreciation for the value of money."

"Harrison bribed a lot of people for me."

"Chivalrous," said Melanie with a touch of sarcasm.

"Under the circumstances," said Julia, an edge to her voice, "it was."

Melanie grinned triumphantly. "See that? You got all defensive over him. You have *got* to tell me what happened between you two."

Julia took a breath. She was suddenly tired, tired of lying, tired of putting on a good front, tired of suppressing her emotions. "We had a fling."

"Aha!"

"You have to keep it quiet."

Melanie nodded eagerly. "I'll absolutely keep it quiet."

"It's important to Harrison. He really is going to propose to somebody." Julia swallowed. "Her name is Brittany."

Melanie waved a dismissive hand. "Brittany, schmit-tany. What happened between the two of you?"

"I don't know," she said, pulling her muffin into two sections. Something about confessing to Melanie had improved her appetite. "Adrenaline?"

"They say it's an aphrodisiac."

"Well, it's something. Or maybe Harrison is some-thing. But whatever it was, it hit us like a ton of bricks at the oasis." Raw memories threatened to swamp her.

"I'm glad it wasn't all danger and intrigue."

Julia forced herself to smile, but it was growing more difficult. "Then back at his palace—" She blinked her burning eyes. "Well, that was—"

Melanie came to her feet, a worried expression on her face. "Julia?"

Oh, no. Julia could feel her chest tightening. She clenched her jaw and fought the rising emotions. But all she could see was Harrison in the palace bedroom, comforting her after her nightmare, kissing her, holding her, making her feel as though an insane world would really be all right after all.

"Julia?" Melanie asked again. "What the hell hap-pened over there?"

Julia looked up at her friend.

Melanie's shoulders slumped. "You fell for him."

Julia nodded miserably.

How, oh, *how* could she have let that happen?

"And he's gone back to propose to another woman?"

"Yes," Julia squeaked out. "She's a lovely woman. She has a title, and she looks like a movie star. And she's nice." A couple of tears escaped, and Julia swiped them away. "She's genuinely nice. I don't blame him for wanting her."

"Do you want to go after him?" asked Melanie.

"No!" Julia frantically shook her head. "That would be a disaster."

"You don't know that."

"Yes, I do. I do. He's a baron. He actually has the title 'The Honorable' in front of his name."

"So what?"

"So *what?*"

"Yeah." Melanie nodded.

"You don't know what he said to me last night."

Melanie waited.

"He said being his wife was a really hard job, and Brittany knew how to do it. She could help both him and their children."

Melanie sat back down. "Oh."

"So, you see. He's gone back to his own world, and I can't go after him."

Melanie didn't seem convinced. "Are you sure he didn't mean—"

"It was pretty clear what he meant."

Melanie slumped back on the couch. "What can I do to help?"

Julia gave a watery smile. "Thanks for listening."

"There's got to be more than that."

"There isn't. But thanks." Julia set the muffin aside. "I think I'll head home now. I hope you get Leopold's Legacy figured out soon."

"This sucks," said Melanie.

"Life does sometimes," said Julia, trying desperately to be tough and pragmatic. "But at least I'm not in a jail cell."

She'd cling to that reality. Even if Harrison hadn't fallen in love with her, he got her out of jail in Dubai, and he saved her life. She'd always be grateful for that.

Chapter Sixteen

Harrison spent most of the trip across the Atlantic telling himself to buck up and be a man about it.

Sure, he'd missed Julia last night. But it was obvious she was ready to walk away, and he'd had no choice but to respect her wishes. Although every minute took him farther away from her, he tried to remind himself he was also heading toward something else, a course of action that would ultimately make the most sense.

But, by the time they crossed the Azores, he knew he had to stop in London. He also knew he had to tell both Brittany and his grandmother the engagement wasn't going to happen. He'd betrayed Brittany in the most fundamental way a man could betray a woman. It wasn't that he'd slept with Julia. Problem was, he'd fallen in love with Julia.

He'd asked his pilot to refile the flight plan, and now they were easing onto the runaway at Heathrow.

He'd also forced himself to go over a backlog of business e-mails, composing answers while they were in the air. Once the jet was taxiing at Heathrow, he hooked up his connection and sent everything off.

There was some good news on the pipeline front. France and Turkmenistan were ready to start formal talks. Harrison would have to be in Paris for that at the end of the month. He'd also contacted a top-notch, international private investigative firm. They'd get started on the investigation around Millions to Spare's death immediately and, hopefully, have some information for the Prestons soon.

His jet stopped at the private boarding gates, and he headed down the gangway into a blustery fall evening in London. There was a limo waiting for him, and he made a few calls while half watching a news station on his way to Brittany's family home near Hyde Park.

"We've arrived, sir," the limo driver informed him as the car came to a halt.

One of the Livingstons' footmen quickly opened Harrison's door, and Harrison thanked him as he got out.

Another staff member greeted him on the lighted, stone porch and offered to announced him to Brittany. The Livingstons had always lived on the formal side, even for the aristocracy, and Harrison couldn't help but contrast their lifestyle to the cozy little cabin where he'd spoken with Julia just last night.

Brittany appeared almost immediately in the marble and gilded entry hall.

"Harrison." She smiled politely, giving him a kiss on the cheek. "How good of you to stop by."

Again, Harrison's brain brought up a contrast to Julia. If he'd arrived unannounced on her doorstep at nine in the evening, she'd probably ask him what the heck he wanted.

"Shall we go into the parlor?" Brittany offered.

"I came to apologize," said Harrison as he fell into step with her. "I'm sorry I had to leave so suddenly."

They crossed through a set of double doors to a dark paneled room with French provincial furniture, heavy oil paintings and ornate, antique crystal chandeliers.

Brittany gestured to a burgundy upholstered chair. "I understand completely," she told him.

He waited for her to sit down in the opposite chair before taking his own seat.

A butler arrived.

"Would you care for a cocktail?" asked Brittany. "Or perhaps some tea?"

"Tea would be nice," said Harrison. "I'm time zone challenged at the moment."

"Of course." She nodded to the butler, who exited the room.

Immediately a trio of maids appeared, setting out cups and spoons, sugar, cream, honey and lemon. Then another maid arrived with a tray of sweets, and yet another with a pot of tea.

Harrison waited until the little flurry had calmed down and Brittany had poured the tea.

He took a sip and nodded his appreciation. "I am sorry our visit in Dubai didn't go as I had planned."

Brittany's cup rattled against the saucer.

He peered closely at her expression and realized she was nervous about something.

He had a horrible thought. Was she expecting him to propose here and now?

"Harrison." She set down her cup.

What could he do?

What could he say?

He didn't want to hurt her.

"There's something I need to discuss with you," she continued.

He set down his own cup and leaned forward, relieved to have her keep talking a little while longer. "Please," he invited.

"This is difficult," she said, smoothing her hair back from her face.

Then she rose, and Harrison quickly rose with her.

She crossed the room and shut the parlor door. Then she turned to face him. "I've always thought we were perfect for each other."

Harrison didn't know what to say to that, but his worst fear seemed to be coming true. He truly didn't want to break Brittany's heart. She was a lovely woman.

"We have so much in common," she continued. "Music, art, religion, politics. And we have so many mutual friends."

He needed to shut this conversation down before she said something that would later prove embarrassing. "I understand how you might—"

She held up a hand to stop him. "I'm sorry. Please. I need to say it all."

Harrison nodded. He had no choice.

"And you and I, far more than most people, understand there's still value in uniting families. A title is important. It's important socially, and it gives children so many advantages in life."

"Brittany, I—"

"I can't marry you, Harrison."

Harrison could swear that his jaw dropped open. He was completely speechless.

"I know it's a foolish decision on my part."

Not foolish at all. She *didn't* want to marry him? Had he heard that right?

"Problem is—" she walked back to her chair and dropped down into it "—I'm in love with someone else."

It was Harrison's turn to drop into his chair. He stared at her, speechless with surprise.

She gave a little laugh. "He's a commoner. He's an American. He's brash and outspoken and opinionated. And he's not the least bit intimidated by my title or my family or pretty much anything for that matter."

She took a breath. "For the first time in my life, I've found someone for whom it's worth defying both my family and convention. Father will rage, as you can imagine."

Harrison could well imagine. "Do you need my help?" he asked her.

She gave him a curious look.

"With your father. I'd be happy to talk to him if you think it would help."

"You're not angry?"

Harrison gave her a smile. "How could I be angry?" He reached out and took both of her hands. "It sounds like you're going to be happy."

Her eyes shimmered, and she blinked rapidly. "Maybe."

"Are you ready to tell me who he is?"

She shook her head. "Not yet. He doesn't..." She glanced away. "He still thinks I'm marrying you."

Harrison smiled at the irony. "I know how that can go."

"I hope we can still be friends." Her voice shook ever so slightly. And no wonder. She was about to embark on a course of action that would rattle the foundations of her family and ripple out into society across London.

"Absolutely," he answered her question. He came to his feet, drawing her up with him, and pulling her into a gentle hug. "I wish you nothing but happiness," he told her. "And I'm here for you in whatever you need. If you need to get out of London for a while. If you need anything financially. And, please, bring him to meet me as soon as you can?"

Brittany gave a strange, little laugh, and it did Harrison's heart good.

He drew back and gave her hand another squeeze. "Well done, Brittany. I'm very proud of you."

And he was.

He was also a little disappointed in himself. Brittany was heading out on a very big limb for her love, whereas he'd given up Julia without the slightest of fights.

Back at his London flat, Harrison stared out the window across the black water of the Thames. He'd picked up the phone to call Julia a dozen times. But he had to find the right words. He knew he only had one shot at this, and he wasn't about to blow it.

A knock sounded on his door, and he crossed the floor to find Alex on the porch.

"What on earth are you doing in London?" Last time Harrison had checked, Alex was still holding down the fort in Dubai.

"I have to talk to you," Alex responded, marching into the square foyer and removing his coat, tossing it on a wall hook.

"It seems to be an epidemic today," Harrison commented as he led the way into the living room. He took his favorite Windsor chair, while Alex walked to the big, bay window and stared out.

Harrison wondered if something was wrong on the pipeline deal. Funny, he couldn't bring himself to care about a financial loss right now.

After a moment, Alex turned. He reached into the breast pocket of his suit and extracted a white envelope. "I'm handing you my resignation."

Harrison couldn't have been more stunned if Alex had pulled out a gun and demanded the silver. "You're *what?*"

"I'm resigning."

Harrison scrambled to make sense of the words. How had this happened? Why hadn't he seen it coming?

Alex took five swift steps across the room and dropped the letter on the lamp table beside Harrison.

Harrison didn't even look at the envelope. "Have you lost your mind?"

Alex shook his head. "I've done something that makes me unfit as your employee."

"Is it serious? Can we solve it? Was it illegal?"

Alex took a very deep breath. "I slept with Brittany."

Harrison's jaw definitely fell open this time.

"I'm in love with her, Harrison. And, fair warning, I'm going to fight you for her."

Harrison came to his feet, struggling to keep his expression serious. An American, Brittany had said. Brash and fearless, who didn't care what her family or anybody else thought.

"You mean fisticuffs?" he asked Alex. "Pistols at dawn? How exactly are we going to fight?"

"Are you *smiling?* Why aren't you going for my throat? I just told you I slept with your fiancée."

"She's not my fiancée."

"Technical point. You're going to marry her." He paused. "For Christ's sake, *why* are you smiling?"

"Because," said Harrison, deciding to put Alex out of his misery, "Brittany just finished telling me she was in love with another man. And three days ago, I married Julia to get her out of the country."

Alex's expression hardened. His eyes crackled with hostility, and his skin tone turned ruddy. "What other man?"

"Relax," said Harrison, finding it intriguing that Alex didn't even react to the Julia story. "Brittany wouldn't give me a name. But I'm guessing it's you."

Alex drew sharply back.

"She said he was a brash, outspoken American who didn't give a damn about her title. Oh, and I asked her if she'd introduce me to him. I guess that explains why she laughed. She also said he still thought she was marrying me. But she's not. She broke it off with me an hour ago."

It took less than a second for Alex to react.

He turned for the door, and Harrison quickly handed him his coat, since he didn't look as if he was about to slow down for anything.

As the door slammed shut, Harrison dropped back down in his chair. Brittany was giving everything up for Alex. And Alex was willing to slay dragons for her.

What was Harrison willing to do to have Julia?

Simple. Anything and everything.

Sipping a second cup of tea in the parlor, Brittany knew she should feel terrible. She should feel nervous and regretful, even fearful of her father's reaction. But she couldn't help it, she felt happy, even light. She felt freer than she could ever remember. There wasn't an ounce of guilt in her at the moment.

"Lady Brittany?" came the butler's voice through the open double doors.

She glanced up.

"A Mr. Lindley is—"

Before the introduction was even complete, Alex was striding through the door.

"Alex." She popped up from her seat, unable to keep a smile from bursting out. Alex was here. He was in London.

"Sir," admonished the butler.

"It's fine, Reginald," Brittany put in. "Please close the door."

To his credit, Alex waited until the door was shut before speaking.

"He's the first thing to go," Alex growled.

"What are you talking about?" She was still grinning.

Alex advanced on her. "Harrison just told me you're in love with an American."

"I am," she admitted, a rush of excitement and anticipation hitting her system.

Alex halted directly in front of her. "And he says you're not marrying him."

"I'm not," she agreed.

"Then, I'm here to ask if you're open to offers."

"I am. You've got an offer to make?"

"Marry me. Thumb your nose at your family. And you'll spend every night of your life in ecstasy."

Her grin widened even farther. "That's a bold offer."

He grinned right back at her. "I'm a bold man."

"My father may challenge you to a duel."

"Tell him I used to kill people professionally and blow things up recreationally. Maybe he'll change his mind."

"I doubt it."

"Then how do you feel about eloping?"

"I'm afraid we're going to have to stay here and face the music."

"Well, I'm not killing your father, and I'm sure not letting him kill me."

"Then we should probably talk to my mother. She's more reasonable, and she's used to calming him down."

Alex was silent for a moment. "Is that a yes, Brittany?"

She slowly nodded.

Alex was the brass ring of happiness. She was marrying him, and nothing was going to stop her. She'd finally found something in her life worth defying her father for.

Alex sobered. He cupped her face and kissed her gently on the mouth. "I don't even have a ring."

"You don't need a ring."

"We're buying one tomorrow. Something huge and ostentatious so your father doesn't think I'm destitute. I'm not destitute, Brittany. I'm not Harrison, but I'm quite wealthy."

"It doesn't matter."

"It does. A little. I want you to know you'll have everything you need."

She kissed him again, wrapping her arms around him to hold him close. "I already have everything I need."

Buying a Dalmatian puppy was just the shot in the arm Julia needed. As she watched Herman scamper across the floor of her condo, slipping to a stop, then valiantly trying to get his little puppy jaws around a blue-and-red-striped ball, she smiled for the first time in two days.

She was still feeling lonely and maudlin whenever she let herself think about Harrison, but Herman was showing her there was light at the end of the tunnel. The puppy books, the gear, the house training and the walks by the river gave her a focus for her life.

She wouldn't be able to travel as much now that she had him, but she'd decided to scale back on her work for *Equine Earth,* and start working freelance on the kinds of investigative stories she'd always wanted to undertake. Life was too short to stay in the lifestyle section.

A knock came on her door.

With a quick check to make sure Herman was occupied and wouldn't dart out, she pulled it open.

She gave her head a shake and blinked to clear her eyes, certain she must be hallucinating Harrison with a Dalmatian puppy in his arms.

"Meet Herman," came the voice that had haunted her dreams.

Behind her, Herman barked and jumped at her calves.

"Uh-oh," said Harrison.

Julia scooped up the puppy, and she couldn't help but smile. "*This* is Herman."

The two puppies barked at one another, desperately trying to get down to play on the floor.

"Come on in," Julia said to Harrison, standing aside, then closing the door behind him before they released the puppies.

They barked and wrestled and chased their way

across the living-room floor. Julia kept her back to Harrison as she watched the puppies play, using the distraction to try to come to terms with his arrival. What was he doing here? What did he want?

After a couple of minutes, his big hands closed over her shoulders. "Hello, Julia."

She struggled to keep the emotion out of her voice. "Hello, Harrison."

"How have you been?"

She shrugged. Fine didn't quite describe it, but she was surviving. "Did you have business in Lexington?"

"No business."

She turned then. "Why are you here?"

"I came to see you."

She forced a light note into her voice, pretending they were mere acquaintances who might see each other from time to time. "You came all the way to Kentucky to bring me a puppy?"

He shook his head.

Then another thought occurred to her. "Did you find out something about Millions to Spare?"

He shook his head again. "I realized," he began. Then his gaze softened, focusing on a spot behind her. "You may have misunderstood. And I need to explain."

She waited for him to elaborate.

"That last night at the Prestons," he said. "When I told you that being my wife was a terrible job...I don't think I put it quite correctly." He took a breath and looked directly into her eyes. "What I meant to say was, it's a terrible job. But will you take it on anyway?"

Julia struggled to make sense of his words. "I don't understand."

"I'm asking you to stay married to me."

"What about Brittany? What about the perfect children?" Julia's mind still couldn't wrap itself around his about-face.

"Brittany's marrying Alex."

"She's *what?*"

Harrison had been jilted? Wow. She'd bet he hadn't seen that one coming.

"Apparently their police chase around UAE was more fun than they expected."

So Julia was second choice? Did Harrison want to marry her because Brittany was unavailable?

She loved him, but could she live with that?

The puppies barked and growled behind her, and she turned to see what they'd gotten into.

"Julia?"

They were pouncing on the rubber ball, and she watched their carefree frolicking for a few minutes.

"Julia?" Harrison tried again.

She sighed and turned back to him. "I can't take Brittany's place."

His brow creased. "Is that what you—"

"I'm sorry."

He raked his hand through his hair. "You're not taking *Brittany's place*," he boomed, and the puppies froze in their play. "Brittany was taking yours. I realized that on my way back home. *I* went to her. *I* was going to tell her I couldn't marry her because I was in love with *you*."

If his indignation was anything to go by, he was completely serious.

Something broke loose inside Julia. He loved her. Harrison actually loved her. She suddenly felt as happy and carefree as the puppies. A smile grew on her face.

Harrison lowered his voice, sincerity rumbling

through it. "I love you, Julia. But I'm not exaggerating, being my wife is a tough job. And I don't want you to—"

"Would people try to kill me very often?" she asked.

He took in her expression and grinned. "We'll have to stay out of Dubai for a while. I'd like to make it clear, though, that they weren't trying to kill you because you were my wife."

"Fair point."

"And, no, I don't expect there will be many threats on your life. Not after the people I've hired finish investigating Muwaffaq, Rafiq and all of their associates. But I have business all over the world."

"I can write stories all over the world."

"I'll change what I can, but I have responsibilities to my companies. The social obligations are huge. There's hosting and entertaining—"

"Did I mention that I speak French?"

He paused. "I believe you did."

"Spanish, too. And I usually know which fork to use."

He chuckled. "That's good. And I'm planning to hire you some help."

"Excuse me?" What was it he thought she needed help with?

"A secretary."

Julia wasn't sure how she felt about that.

"I had Leila in mind," he elaborated.

Oh. Julia could definitely live with that.

"One last question," she told him. "Are we going to have to go through one of those cathedral weddings to satisfy your family? Because I'm really not wild about—"

"How does this sound?" He closed on her, wrapping his arms loosely around her waist. "'Baron Welsmeire is pleased to announce his marriage to American journalist Julia Nash in a private ceremony at his palace in Dubai. The two met at the Sandstone Derby at Nad Al Sheba racecourse earlier this year. The couple plans to honeymoon in the South Pacific prior to taking up residence at the Rochester Estate in Windsor.'"

She smiled, and he leaned in to give her a gentle kiss.

"Where they'll raise Dalmatian puppies," she added, "plant a cherry orchard and travel far and wide on their diplomatic passports."

He slipped his arms fully around her waist and drew her close. "That sounds absolutely perfect. But there's one last thing."

"Yes?"

"Do you love me, Julia?"

She nodded, meaning the words with all her heart. "Yes. I love you, Harrison. I love you very, very much."

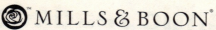

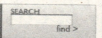

Romantic reads to
Need, Want

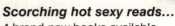

LOOK OUT...

...for this month's special product offer.
It can be found in the envelope
containing your invoice.

**Special offers are exclusively for
Mills & Boon® Book Club members.**

You will benefit from:

- Free books & discounts
- Free gifts
- Free delivery to your door
- No purchase obligation – 14 day trial
- Free prize draws

THE LIST IS ENDLESS!!

*So what are you waiting for —
take a look NOW!*

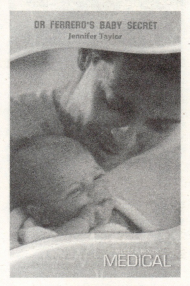